AIDAN HALE is thirty-eight years of age. He lives and works in Coventry with his lovely wife, Sandra, and has four children, Sandra, Mandy, Jimmy and little Katie.

His love of writing began at school, but it wasn't until he started a writing course with the Writers Bureau that the seeds of this novel began.

Juggling his time between writing, work commitments and family, he began this novel by combining a course assignment with his love of horror.

TROOPER

TROOPER

Aidan M D Hale

ATHENA PRESS
LONDON

TROOPER

ISBN 10-digit: 1 84401 943 8
ISBN 13-digit: 978 1 84401 943 4

First Published 2007 by
ATHENA PRESS
Queen's House, 2 Holly Road
Twickenham TW1 4EG
United Kingdom

Printed for Athena Press

Acknowledgements

I would like to thank my Dad for making this possible, Sandra for believing in me, Sylvia Blanthorn and Sam for searching the Internet whenever I asked. A special thanks to Nicola Reddington for easing my mind. Peter Whitbread for his patient and expert criticism (without whom none of this would have been possible), Iron Maiden for providing me with escapism as a child and my mum – the best writer I know. It's been a long time coming, but this one's for you.

Prologue

Moving silently, Jack used the bleak night to conceal his movements. Crouched low, they approached the camp, seeing the trucks loaded with the pillaged ivory. They hadn't moved far when the area was suddenly flooded with blinding light. Each man became trapped like a rabbit, frozen in the glare. 'Welcome,' a voice boomed, 'to a *danse macabre*!'

As the first shots rang out, hysteria ensued as Jack's men began blindly returning fire. Each man was singled out, cut down in a massacre, forcing Jack to make a retreat. Glancing back, he was consumed with guilt for leaving them behind.

Getting back to the vehicles was a priority, and, as Jack moved, he was painfully aware of the screams of the dying. Scrambling into one of the waiting Land Rovers, he noticed someone sitting in the passenger seat, unmoving. Immediately he saw a pair of headlights coming towards him. Turning the ignition, the engine rumbled into life, his foot slamming down hard on the accelerator as he reversed. Switching his headlights on full, the oncoming vehicle backed off just enough for him to spin the Land Rover round in a 180-degree turn.

The road abruptly ended before him in an expanse of thick jungle. Banging his foot down harder on the pedal, Jack broke through the dense foliage, ploughing a path through the thicket. Suddenly the vehicle lost all traction and began to drop, the Land Rover sliding out of control until it came to a sudden, stomach-wrenching stop. Dazed and shaken, Jack was still aware of gunfire coming from above when his passenger abruptly turned his head, saying, 'That was some ride, boss!'

Jack was shocked. 'Christ! Bolo, you're alive…'

Bolo smiled, revealing white teeth. 'I thought we were goners back there, boss.'

Jack felt a certain amount of relief that someone had survived, but more so that he was not alone. Staring into the darkness, he said. 'So did I.'

Breaking dawn rapidly approached, giving Jack his first glimpse of the terrain. Sheer banks ran on either side of them. 'Have you any idea where we are?' Jack asked.

'I think we're in a ravine about fifty miles north-west of the reserve, close to the border.'

Jack tried the two-way radio. 'Dead!' he said, throwing the microphone at the dashboard. 'Do you know if there's anywhere we can get help?'

'I can't be sure…' Bolo spoke with caution. 'If memory serves me right there's a Yoruba village round here. I have not been there since I was a boy and…' He became reserved, his eyes frightened.

Jack noticed Bolo's hesitation. 'What's wrong?' he asked.

'They say it bad place, use bad medicine. They say it Vodun village.'

Jack thought the loss of his men was bad medicine. He had led them into a trap and paid the price. He turned the key in the ignition, but the engine was dead.

'Well, we're not going anywhere in this; engine's shot. Bad place or not, we don't have a choice.'

Forced to leave the Land Rover, they continued on foot, as drums sounded in the west, reaching a crescendo. The fevered beat led them on, a small beacon of hope amid the desperation of their situation. They followed the drums across dry scrubland to the edge of the jungle.

The village was small, comprised of a few grass huts. A small native boy stood silently observing their approach. The villagers were gathered, fervently dancing, like they were possessed.

'What are they doing?' Jack asked.

Bolo looked at him, fear residing in his eyes. 'Allowing the spirits of the dead to possess the bodies of the living!'

'Like in voodoo?'

'Like in Vodun!'

The boy followed them, stopping beside Jack. He shouted and the drumming ceased as the entire village stopped to stare at them. A powerful-looking man, his face streaked with mud, approached, addressing Bolo in his native tongue. 'You are not wanted here,' he shouted. 'Go!' He began to violently shake as the shrill sound of a mortar shell resounded around them. Jack's instinct was to grab the boy as the first explosion ripped through the village.

Fire rained down around him, the explosion throwing him through the air. In his arms, the small boy's body was limp and lifeless. Hitting the ground, he felt his ribs crack and he glanced up at a shimmering sun emerging above the horizon. Silhouetted in its glow was the form of a large man wearing a hat, a man he knew to be responsible for the attack – and instinct told him that he was laughing. Then the world went black.

As he opened his eyes, a face hovered above, studying him with eyes of malice.

Chapter 1

Jack struggled within the grasp of sleep's death-like embrace; contesting his own mortality, he was drowning in a pool of his own subconscious phantasms. The moment he opened his eyes he became lost. Lying on his back, looking up at a whitewashed ceiling, a strong smell of antiseptic assailing his nostrils, his memories were vague, and he grasped at them voraciously.

As realisation slowly dawned, Jack became painfully aware of a void within him, a missing piece of his persona that was to be forever denied.

He remembered with clarity the events that had brought him here. Sergeant Jack Hornsby, formally of the prestigious SAS, was now a broken man. A single instant had reduced his world to rubble. He had nearly died in the attempt to save another, and he now wished that he had.

Returning to England, Jack had suffered a relapse of his injuries and was rushed to a military hospital. Now he felt as if he had been written off, a specimen for the doctors to paw over and discuss, like he wasn't there. He felt low: in fact, he could sink no lower.

Confined to an isolation ward, Jack was aware that a nurse observed him through the glass window. Gone was the tent that had encapsulated him for the past thirty days. He'd also noticed that the doctors and nurses were no longer garbed in biological suits. They came and went much the same as they did in the rest of the hospital.

Rising from her seat, the nurse entered. 'How are you feeling today, Jack?' Her smile held an illumination that brightened his bleak surroundings. Jack had discovered that although hospital intentions were honourable, they were as unsympathetic and cold as they were clinical.

'All right I suppose… considering,' Jack replied, despondently.

The nurse approached taking hold of his right wrist, feeling for a pulse. There was none, and Jack wanted answers.

As he looked into her sparkling eyes, she whispered, 'I shouldn't be telling you this, but you might be getting out of here soon.'

The words gripped his attention. 'Please continue…' he prompted.

'Well, they now believe your condition to be non-infectious!'

I could have told them that, Jack thought. 'I was a victim of a mortar shell, not an unknown tropical disease,' he said.

She laughed, tossing her head back provocatively and highlighting her fine and delicate chin. 'No, but you were dead on arrival, which the doctors now believe was a deep catatonic state. Your wounds would have been enough to kill any man.'

'Or woman!' Jack added with a smile.

She cast him a woeful stare. 'You were in the mortuary for thirty-six hours!'

Jack became thoughtful. 'It's not like it hasn't happened before. I mean, mistakes can be made. People have woken up in their coffins, been buried alive…'

'And you want to thank your lucky stars that you were not one of them!'

Giving a weak laugh, Jack said, 'Fat chance! I've left strict instructions that I want to be cremated.'

She leaned closer to Jack. 'I overheard Captain Warner saying the finest medical minds in the country are in a quandary, which is why you are still on twenty-four-hour watch.'

Reading between the lines, Jack gleaned a small amount of hope – hope that he could get out of this antiseptic hellhole, although there was now a question mark by his name and likewise his career.

Giving a faltering smile, he said, 'An honourable discharge. It seems that my use to the British Army has run its course!'

Unknown to both of them, a tall man with dark hair immaculately presented observed them from the open doorway. He cleared his throat loudly.

'I think this conversation has ended,' he said curtly, giving the young nurse a scalding glance. 'I'll be having words with you later.'

He allowed his gaze to remain on the nurse long enough to

make her feel uncomfortable before turning his attention back to Jack. His smile was almost friendly. 'Well Jack, how are you feeling?'

'Fine!'

'Good, good…' He averted his gaze momentarily. 'No headaches?' Jack shook his head. 'Joints and muscles feel fine? Any diarrhoea, vomiting, sore throat or hiccups?' Again, Jack shook his head.

Although the doctor looked directly at him, Jack couldn't help feeling that the man was looking through him, evaluating him for his parts as opposed to his personality.

'Look, Doc, I just want to know when I can get out of here.'

Jack saw plainly the man's discomfort. Shunning Jack's question, he referred to his notes. 'That is a topic we will discuss at a more appropriate time.'

Colonel Oliver Windburn placed his hands behind his head and leant back in his chair. He casually glanced around him at the familiar surroundings; each item in the room told a story, like a pictorial account of his military career.

The Colonel was a man heading towards his twilight years; his hair had begun to grey and he wore a weathered and tired face. The report that lay on the desk puzzled him. It was an accurate enough account, but the Colonel felt that it was missing something – a vital key that would unlock a mystery that lay hidden within the words.

The Colonel was a professional man with an uncanny ability to infiltrate the minds of the men that served under his command. He read one line of the report repeatedly.

'It was an ambush, and I had led all my men to their deaths with the exception of Bolo.'

This self-blame was not like Jack Hornsby at all. The Colonel knew Jack to be a solid man, a man of integrity and honour. He was a lateral thinker. The Colonel had likened him to a detective in his thought processes and analysis of problems. It had been this reason that made him the perfect choice to place as a sleeper. Not only had Jack had the training to blend in with his surroundings, but he could also probe into the varying scenarios that would inevitably confront him.

The Colonel re-read the report, trying to gain an insight into Jack's mind. He had gleaned from the handwritten pages that Jack had walked into an ambush and that the individuals involved were more than what they had at first appeared. His mind made up, the Colonel decided that he had to go and see Jack himself.

Jack lay on the bed, his eyes closed against the clinical scenery that was serving to pull him into melancholy. Automatically, his remaining senses had heightened, making him fully aware of his surroundings. He heard the swish of a door and the crisp click of heels on the highly polished floor. They stopped at his bedside. Jack opened his eyes as Captain Warner's educated, upper-crust accent cut in.

'Hello, Jack. There is someone here to see you – a Colonel Windburn.'

Jack sat up, intrigued that the old man would bother to make a personal visit. He knew the type of man the Colonel was: methodical, not someone to rush head-on into a situation. He would always evaluate all collected intelligence before making an informed move. He knew there were small holes in his report, holes that, when filled in, would offer a wider and broader picture. Captain Warner informed Jack that the Colonel would see him in his office.

Knocking on the door, Jack was greeted with a crisp, 'Enter.' He walked in to be confronted by a man sitting on the corner of the desk. He was dressed in combat fatigues, with a sand-coloured beret perched on his head. There was no indication of the man's rank except for the famous flamed sword that was pinned to his beret, but to Jack there was no mistaking the wizened, old, weathered face of the Colonel. Jack saluted him.

'Sit down Jack, will you?' The calm demeanour in the Colonel's voice made the order sound more like a request.

Jack complied, positioning himself comfortably in a chair and studying the compelling person who was seated before him.

'How long's it been since you joined the regiment, Jack?'

'Six years, boss.'

The Colonel smiled and nodded his head, glancing down at an

array of papers he had positioned on the desktop, talking as he read. 'The last two years you have been posted in Cameroon, using the Waza National Park as your cover. You were a game warden?'

'Head warden,' Jack corrected. This brought a smile to the Colonel's lips.

'Yes, you engaged a group of supposed poachers who, you imply in your report, were more than you originally deduced?'

'Normal poachers – that is, the natives who work for illegal ivory traders – will not usually engage in any type of gunplay unless forced to do so. What was different in this case was that the men we were following lay in ambush.'

The Colonel studied Jack's eyes.

'I should have known that I was dealing with something that was out of the norm. The casings I found lying around were of a high calibre, not the usual run-of-the-mill stuff that you become used to when dealing with poachers. They were precision casings, military hardware. This aroused my suspicions so I pursued. I wanted to get a bearing on whom or what I was dealing with.'

The Colonel nodded again, looking down at the report. 'And the ambush?'

Jack's face was strained as he forced his mind back. 'Jungle stood before us; a single game trail led away from the plane…' Jack stopped, and the Colonel watched him as sweat appeared on his brow. Jack's eyes were far away.

'We followed them on foot, after I had conducted a small recon. I thought the area was clear; that was when they sprung their trap…'

The Colonel observed that it was now causing Jack great distress to recall events – a typical symptom in commanding officers who had lost their men during battle. The Colonel rubbed his hand across his head, all the time his eyes never leaving Jack's. 'And you got no indication of who these people were?'

'Didn't get a look. Everything happened too fast, though my gut told me that they weren't poachers!'

The Colonel nodded his head as Jack asked, 'What is to happen to me now?'

The Colonel's eyes drifted to the desk where Jack's medical report lay: SUBJECT UNFIT FOR DUTY AND WILL REMAIN SO UNTIL FURTHER NOTICE.

'I can't say for certain Jack until I have talked with the doctors...' His head lowered. The Colonel hated to lose a good man. 'To be blunt, it doesn't look good.' He could feel Jack's anguish and knew that he was looking for answers from him.

After Jack had left the office, the Colonel was studying the medical report when there was a sudden knock at the door. He looked up as Captain Warner walked in. 'Sir?'

'I just wanted us to have a bit of an informal chat. I've been reviewing Hornsby's medical records...' He watched as Captain Warner's eyes drifted to the document on the desk and frowned. 'I understand that it's not common practice to share these records... But I must stipulate that this is an unusual case, and I would like you to tell me in layman's terms Jack's precise condition.'

Warner was momentarily silent. He looked from the open document to the face of the Colonel.

'Sergeant Jack Hornsby's condition is unique. I have never come across anything like it. To put it bluntly, the man should be dead. I became involved with the case after they found Sergeant Hornsby alive in the mortuary, three days after he had been diagnosed as clinically dead. I deduced that he had been in a deep catatonic state. His wounds had reopened. At first, my conclusion was that he was suffering from a rare type of Ebola haemorrhagic fever. I concluded this due to the man having returned from Africa, though there have been no recorded cases of Ebola HF in Cameroon.

'He was suffering from reddening of the eyes and a rash, and complained of a headache and a sore throat. These symptoms were shortly followed by stomach pains, vomiting and diarrhoea. Early diagnoses in Ebola cases can be difficult; the incubation period can be from two to twenty-one days, which is why the patient had to be isolated. After informing the District Health Authority and Chief Medical Officer, I submitted blood and tissue samples to the Consultant in Communicable Disease Control (CCDC).'

'But they found no signs of the virus?' the Colonel added, reading from the report.

'The CCDC found no trace of viral infection or disease. In

fact, I received a strong telephone call implying that I was playing some kind of prank. The samples received were of a perfectly healthy individual, with one exception: they showed slight traces of cellular breakdown and could not possibly have come from a live patient.'

The Colonel looked quizzically at the Captain. 'Meaning?'

'Jack's body is decomposing. Bacteria that are normally dormant until after death are active in Jack. Now, this decay is minuscule, at a cellular level – hardly noticeable. The CCDC lab suggested the subject could have been dead for an hour or up to a maximum of three days.' The Captain paused allowing the Colonel to digest what he was telling him. 'At the present rate, assuming that the decay stays the same, then I estimate that he will be a walking skeleton within eighteen months.'

'Does he know?'

Captain Warner shook his head. 'Sergeant Hornsby insists that he is fine. In fact, physically, he is in tip-top form, but how long that will last I cannot say... I need time. This is a fascinating case, but if I don't find a way to stop it, then time is something Jack has very little of.'

The Colonel's eyes drifted from the Captain to the report again. 'It mentions here that he is suffering from delusions?'

'Yes.'

'Then you're suggesting that he is mentally impaired?'

Captain Warner's face appeared tense as if he was considering his answer. 'Apart from Jack's unique condition, he is suffering from flashbacks of the attack... Whether this is affecting his attitude I don't know.'

The Colonel looked up. 'Attitude?'

'You must understand, sir, that in no way is my opinion professional. I am a doctor and physician. If you want an opinion on his mental state then I suggest you speak to Lieutenant Howard. This is more his field than mine.'

The Colonel closed the files before him. 'Well, thank you for your time Captain.'

'If that will be all, sir, then I do have other patients who need my attention.'

He stood up and saluted, when the Colonel said, 'I don't have to remind you, Captain, that this information is bound by the official secrets act and any information that leaks will rest squarely on your shoulders.'

Captain Warner tried to protest. 'But Sergeant Hornsby's condition could have a global impact on medicine—'

The Colonel brought the Captain's outburst to a halt with a raised hand. 'That will be all, Captain. Dismissed!'

Captain Warner turned on his heels and left the office. Colonel Windburn closed the file and wrote on the front of the folder beneath Jack's name, RECOMMEND RELIEVED OF ALL DUTIES ON MEDICAL GROUNDS.

Chapter 2

It was drizzling with rain when Jack arrived at work – a humble, fourteen-storey inner-city office block nestled within the scaled metropolis of London. London had never been one of Jack's favourite locations in the world: the hustle and bustle of everyday civilian life hemmed him in.

Jack had been working in London for six months after being released from the hospital. He wasn't cured of his strange illness, but the symptoms seemed to have subsided.

'The condition has become dormant!' Captain Warner had told him and ordered Jack to attend the hospital at regular intervals. The Colonel had arranged for him to work with a security firm that mainly consisted of ex-SAS members. The work was varied, but to Jack's mind it was humdrum and boring. Jack had hoped that when he retired from the regiment he would be able to relax in the knowledge that he had secured himself a place in Africa.

He looked around him, turning his collar up against the biting wind, his despondency deepening along with the weather. Jack still craved the wide, open spaces of that enigmatic continent stretching around him.

Dismal daylight clung to the city – a discouraging omen of more rain to come. For late May, it was cold, and a blustery wind penetrated everything. Jack entered a building through twin stained glass doors. His focus was on a man seated behind a semi-circular reception desk. The man looked up, grinning. 'Evening, Jack!'

'Morning, John!' Jack smiled as he approached the desk. The two men had been friends since Jack had joined the security firm and they had worked together on a previous job.

'Ready for the graveyard shift?' John enquired.

Jack gave a quick smile, trying to overcome his despondency. 'As ready as I'll ever be! I gave that pub you told me about a try at the weekend. Nice little place, isn't it?'

'It is that, and the only place in the suburbs you can find a decent pint of real ale!' John gave a nod and a wink. 'Oh, that reminds me! We had a communiqué this morning, alerting us to be on the lookout for anyone acting strangely.'

'Oh,' Jack said, frowning. 'Why, what's gone down?'

John shook his head, looking at a piece of paper headed, 'memo'.

'All I know is that certain high-level and confidential information has fallen into the hands of one of Bradshaw & Wilkins' competitors. Allegations have been flying around all day. As you can imagine, it has created quite a stir for us!'

'Whose shift was it?' Jack asked.

John perused the report. 'It happened over the weekend. The report is here on the desk if you want to look. As for me, I'm off for a hot date with a fiery redhead.' Jack watched him as he put his coat on. 'I'll see you in the morning and give you all the sordid little details then.'

Watching John leave, Jack sat down, picked up the report and scanned through it briefly. His attention was drawn to a bank of monitors on the far wall. All the security cameras were switched on, showing nothing of particular interest with the exception of one. The security camera for Bradshaw & Wilkins showed a light shining out into a darkened corridor. Jack thought that the cleaners could have left a light on, but he felt it warranted investigation. Checking the log to see if anybody was still on the premises, he found none. Only twice had Jack experienced anybody staying much past 8 p.m.

Suspicion began to grow inside him, and he selected a bunch of keys from a drawer and proceeded towards the elevators. He kept a close eye on the monitor bank whilst waiting. The picture was inferior, displaying a grainy black and white image.

Jack heard the ring of a bell as the elevator came to a gentle stop and the doors slid open. He stepped out onto the fifth floor, checking the corridor. With the exception of the low-wattage nightlights, all was cast in dark shadow. The entrance to Bradshaw & Wilkins stood to Jack's right, the company insignia emblazoned in gold upon the double doors. Jack now clearly saw where the light originated and noted that the alarm had not been set. He tried the door and discovered that it was locked. His suspicions raised, Jack silently pushed a master key into the lock, disengaging the catch. He could hear a muffled conversation involving two people, a man and a woman. The woman sounded upset, almost frightened. As Jack proceeded forward he listened intently.

'I-I-I don't think this is right, Mr Morris. Perhaps I was a bit hasty in accepting your offer.'

The male voice was strong and commanding. 'You come from a poor family, don't you, Cathy? A family that relies on your meagre income. If you do as I say, then you will do very well in this company. If you don't... Well, I'm informed that unemployment is on the rise once again, and who knows how long it will be before you get another job?'

Jack knew the voice, it belonged to Dean Morris, Bradshaw & Wilkins' accountant; the man was a bully, thinly disguised by an air of self-indulgent authority.

Jack realised that he had to re-evaluate his position. The man had a right to be where he was. He could have been working late and neglected to inform security. A muffled sob came from the room, overriding Jack's deliberations. He stormed in.

A young woman was in the process of unbuttoning her blouse. Dean Morris was sitting comfortably next to the door. He held in his hand a tall glass of wine. A second glass, untouched, stood upon a desk. The woman looked at Jack, her face displaying her embarrassment. She was crying.

'Are you all right, miss?' Jack asked.

She offered no reply, casting her gaze downwards as Jack turned his attention upon the seated accountant.

Morris glared at Jack. 'What do you think you are doing?' he asked with an indignant tone.

'My job!' came Jack's taut reply. 'You neglected to inform security that you were still in the building.' Glancing over at the woman Jack added, 'And now I can see why!'

Morris smiled coldly. 'This woman is a criminal. You received the report stating that confidential information had been sold to our competitors. Well, she is the culprit!' The seated man's face became flushed. 'And... and... I was just... interrogating her!'

Jack smiled at the accountant's almost comical performance. 'From what I heard and saw when I came in here, it seemed less like interrogation and more like intimidation. But I have to take your word for it. I'll have to call this in.' Jack observed that both the girl and Morris became frightened.

Standing up the accountant approached Jack. 'Is there really any need for that?'

Jack watched him. 'I know what I saw and there are laws against that kind of thing.'

'You can't talk to me like that!' Morris blustered. Then he grinned in a smug manner. 'I'll have your job for this!'

'I'm sorry, Mr Morris, but I'm calling this in.' As Jack turned, he saw that the girl was looking small and afraid. Her wide eyes flitted from Jack to Morris. 'Are you sure you're OK, miss?' She nodded her head. 'Now, if you would both like to follow me, we'll get this all sorted out.'

As Jack stepped out of the room, he felt strange. Missing his footing, he stumbled forward. This mishap did not go unnoticed by Dean Morris.

'A bit unsteady there, Jack?' Jack looked up through blurred vision. He felt as if he were on a merry-go-round that was going faster and faster. His footing was unsteady and Dean Morris watched him intently.

The elevator door began to slide open; Jack peered inside. The air wavered as a young boy materialised within. Jack blinked. He knew this boy. Stumbling forward in an attempt to grasp him, his hearing was assailed by the rapid tempo of native drums. Closing his eyes, he opened them again to discover an empty elevator car. Nausea swiftly descended, leaving him feeling alone, the haunting beat of the drums pounding in his ears as everything began to swim around him.

A void surrounded Jack, but he sensed that he was not alone. There were others here too, phantoms that moved within the dark, blinded by the pit of damnation. He could perceive things stroking past him, reaching out with dark claws that tried to ensnare him, binding him to them for all of eternity. Jack knew that these phantoms had once been human. He felt different, as though he didn't belong, recognising that he was still flesh and bone, while the other spectres were nothing more than mere suggestions of their former existences.

Opening his eyes, he saw two faces peering down at him, a man and a woman. As realisation dawned, Jack saw the woman's hand clasped across her mouth. Dean Morris had a triumphant sneer etched on his face. 'You should leave the booze alone, Jack!' he stated, speaking with all the piety of a poker player with a winning hand.

Jack stood up. He knew that alcohol was still apparent on his breath.

'Drunk on the job, Jack? That's instant dismissal. I've known for some time about your drinking habit.'

Jack felt he wanted to argue his case, but explaining to Morris would be a pointless cause.

The woman had tried to make herself as inconspicuous as possible, drawing herself into the corner of the elevator. Morris maintained eye contact and said, 'It seems we are at an impasse; you with your little indiscretion, and me with mine.'

Jack's eyebrows arched. 'What are you trying to say, Mr Morris?'

Morris smiled. 'Come now! You seem an intelligent man. Perhaps we can come to a suitable arrangement that could benefit both parties?'

'You scratch my back and I'll scratch yours, you mean?' The distaste in Jack's voice was evident.

'Exactly!' Morris said, smugly.

Jack's mind dwelt on the events of the previous night. He had not succumbed to Morris's veiled offer of salvation. Instead he had done the right thing, calling the incident in to his headquarters. The police had been contacted, and Jack had faced hours of questions, after which he had been eliminated from their inquiries.

His mind kept wandering back to the incident in the elevator. Had he really experienced it, or was his mind now beginning to degenerate?

Lying on top of his bed, Jack listened to the birds singing sweetly outside his window. Closing his eyes, he knew that sleep would yet again elude him.

Instead of sleep, his heartbeat slowed into nothingness, his breathing became non-existent. To any observer, he was, to all intents and purposes, dead. It was during these moments of meditative death that he was freed of his bodily constraints. A core part of his essence would drift around the room, observing his body upon the bed below, and Jack always sensed a primordial force lying in wait just beyond his range of perception.

Maintaining regular contact with the hospital was necessary, but to Jack the prospect of being re-admitted was something he wanted to avoid at all costs. Jack remembered the last conversation he had with Captain Warner. He had told Jack that his condition was unique. There had been no other reported cases, therefore no information, textbook or other wise, could be found. The only thing that the Captain and the CCDC team did know was that there was no known cure. To Jack it seemed that the medical body was waiting for him to decompose so that they could dissect and probe at will.

As Jack pondered on his thoughts, a pounding reached his ears. At first he feared he was having a relapse of the previous night – the drums were still beating in his head – but soon realised the pounding was someone at the front door.

Approaching the door, he opened it to be confronted by Colonel Oliver Windburn. He smiled affably. 'Hello, Jack.'

Jack was fazed. 'Hello, boss,' he said automatically, falling back into his SAS jargon. Jack had not seen Colonel Oliver Windburn in just over six months.

'You're a difficult man to track down.' He held out his hand, which Jack took in a firm shake, although his eyes narrowed with suspicion.

'Track me down! Why would you want to track me down?'

The Colonel gave a wry smile. He knew indirectly that Jack had blamed him for ending his military career.

'Blunt and to the point. Can we go inside?'

Jack watched the Colonel become drenched by the rain. He stood aside and the Colonel walked in, brushing away droplets of water from his shoulder. 'So how's life treating you?'

'It's not what I wanted, nor what I had planned, but I get by… Why are you here?' Jack asked. 'Or, more precisely, what do you want?'

The Colonel was aware of Jack's hostility. 'Straight and to the point! What makes you think I want anything?'

Jack laughed. 'You didn't come all this way in the pouring rain for a chit-chat and a cup of tea!'

The Colonel smiled. 'You're right. I have come to make you a proposition. I am placing no pressure upon you, but would like you to hear me out. Something's come up, Jack. But first I would like to tell you a story.' Uninvited, he settled himself into an armchair.

'My initiation into the SAS came late in life. I had served in the ranks of the Royal Fusiliers for fifteen years. What made me want to join I can't exactly say, except maybe it was that I wanted to make a difference.

'Your father was my initial Staff Sergeant and told me that I didn't have a cat in hell's chance of making it through selection. Well, I proved him wrong, much to his approval, I might add. At that time, I had friends in intelligence circles, and, instead of serving my two years, which is every officer's duty in the ranks of the regiment, it was decided that I would be kept on as a liaison officer for the Defence Intelligence Staff. In my official capacity I would assess and personally select certain regimental individuals for special services to our country. You see, intelligence circles such as SIS and GCHQ saw the SAS as a greater asset than just counter-insurgence and counter-terrorism. You were one such individual that possessed the required attributes that would be of benefit to both military and intelligence services.'

Jack held up his hand, shaking his head. 'Hold on, hold on. What has this got to do with me? In fact, what makes you think I give a damn? Remember, I am burnt out – a man with a condition that nobody's got a fucking name for; a man drummed out of the life he knew and loved—' Jack's eyes became mere pinpricks as he looked down to a table that held a bottle of whiskey, which he picked up and brandished before the Colonel. 'Reduced to this because of his condition. You're asking me to become part of the firm again. Well, remember one thing, sir…' – Jack placed emphasis on his formal address of the Colonel – 'The firm turned its back on me, not the other way around!'

The Colonel began to think that maybe he had made a mistake in coming, when Jack said, 'I could drink ten bottles of this stuff and it wouldn't faze me a bit. What is wrong with me?' Jack allowed his outburst to taper off. The Colonel, although filled with remorse, knew that he could show none of his emotion.

'I'm sorry, Jack. It seems that maybe I've made a mistake.' He made to get up and watched Jack as he held his head in his hands.

'No! It's me who is sorry. Call it pressures of civilian life. Please sit down, and I'll listen to what you have to say.'

'I never like to admit when I'm wrong, Jack, but this time I may have made an error in judgement.'

Jack smiled weakly. 'If I said I'd had a bad day at work, would that make any difference? Please continue.'

The Colonel studied Jack closely. 'To get to the point, Jack, we need a man in Africa. Someone who knows the lie of the land and its customs. Someone who can think on their feet. I won't mince my words. It's dangerous and you'll be on your own.'

Jack sat down in the armchair opposite the Colonel – his attention had been seized. 'It's not like I haven't been there before, boss.'

The Colonel gave a half-smile. 'You have to understand, Jack, you'll be going in on your own, and if you get out…'

'I'll be on my own!' Jack finished for him. 'Why me?'

'Because we need a man of exceptional prowess. I felt – feel – that you could be that man.'

Jack thought about what had been said to him for a moment.

'Won't my illness be a liability?'

The Colonel took a deep breath; this was the only compromise in his plan. Before he had sought Jack out, he had known what sort of man he was. But now, after six months of living with his condition, he was unsure of Jack's mental stability. His doubts were reinforced by Jack's outburst. The Colonel cleared his throat.

'Jack, I have to be honest, after seeing you now, I'll admit I have doubts. But my gut instinct is telling me otherwise. So you tell me – are my doubts unfounded?'

Jack smiled. 'You mean, am I the burnout that I'm portraying myself to be? I'll never know unless I take you up on your offer. So tell me, what exactly are you offering?'

'The chance to go anywhere you wish – to remain in Africa if you want! A chance to rebuild your life and start again.'

Jack looked around him at the small ground floor maisonette and all of its meagre contents. He was also aware that he mightn't have a job in the morning. Did the Colonel know about last night's events? And, if he did, how long had he been keeping tabs on Jack? Jack had to admit that the timing of his offer had been precise. Jack smiled, offering his hand out in acceptance. 'I'm in, boss.'

Colonel Windburn studied Jack intently. 'You understand that I must satisfy myself that you are the man for this job, Jack. I will give you twenty-four hours to set your affairs straight, then I want you to report to Bradbury Lines.' He handed Jack a folded document. 'Give them this.' The Colonel rose from his seat. 'You used to be one of the best, Jack, and I am hoping that you still are.'

Jack sensed the pride that was conveyed in the Colonel's remark. He had always held a great respect for the man. In some respects, he had come to think of the Colonel as a substitute father. Jack's natural father was still alive – he had served in the same regiment – yet the two men were total opposites. Jack rapidly brought himself out of his thoughts as the Colonel walked to the front door. 'I'll let myself out, Jack.'

Chapter 3

As Jack drove to Hereford, he was full of expectation, like a child coming home from their first trip away.

Entering Herefordshire, he found himself driving along familiar roads, roads he had not travelled in many years. He observed signs that were placed to deter civilians from wandering into restricted areas, and he was sure that eyes, unseen, would be monitoring his progress: troopers out on manoeuvres, reporting back to HQ. This was the heart of SAS operations, and they could take him out like the snapping of fingers, if the order was given.

Jack could see a sentry post ahead of him; three armed men in combat fatigues were standing behind the closed barrier. Jack brought his vehicle to a gradual standstill. As he lowered his window, the tallest of the three approached. 'Can't you fucking read?' he said. 'This is government property! Off limits!' The man had a Scouse accent, thin and rangy, not exactly the type of person you would expect to be SAS.

'My name's Jack Hornsby. I'm expected!' Jack handed over the documentation the Colonel had given him before his departure.

The Scouser studied his face intently, his stare steadfast and unwavering. 'Jack Hornsby?' he enquired. 'Sergeant Jack Hornsby?'

'Yes.'

'Will you follow me, please? My orders are to escort you back to barracks. You can leave your car here.'

The barrier was raised and Jack followed the trooper to a waiting Land Rover.

The Land Rover drove through miles of countryside, the interior silent as no conversation transpired between him and his escort. Jack blinked, catching a glimpse of an African boy standing at the side of the road. The boy beckoned to him as Jack felt the panic stir inside. The boy was nothing more than a figment of his imagination. There were no civilians allowed here.

Trying to make the vision go away, he blinked again, but the boy remained as they passed within feet of him. Quickly turning, the apparition vanished like smoke.

When they came to a standstill, Jack heard the sounds of rapid gunfire. 'Mock hijack,' the trooper stated. 'Never know when you'll be called to perform another Iranian Embassy job!'

Jack's wait for the Colonel was longer than he had anticipated. In that time, he had not been left idle. The Colonel had left strict orders that Jack was to be kept busy. He was in the gym lifting weights when he was notified that the Colonel wanted to see him in the debriefing room.

Jack walked the long corridor feeling like he was fresh off a two-week leave. The acute click of his heels rang off the walls as he approached a partially open door. He overheard voices from inside that petered out at his approach. Pausing, he gave a sharp knock that opened the door wider. He did not enter until told to do so.

The debriefing room was sparse, with the exception of a cluster of chairs that sat before a table. A screen had been located in the centre of one wall and a projector sitting on the table before it.

The Colonel was seated behind the table; two of the chairs were occupied opposite him, and there was a fourth person, a young man with defined stubble, who was standing next to the window smoking a cigarette. Jack looked at each face in turn, inwardly making visual evaluations of each one. One thing was common to all: their faces remained lacklustre. 'Jack!' the Colonel said as he entered. 'I hope you've not been bored since your arrival?'

Jack grinned. 'Far from it, but then you probably know that!'

The Colonel smiled back. Jack approached the table and perched himself on the corner. Familiarity in the regular ranks of the army was taboo, but the SAS had a more informal approach to protocol.

The Colonel continued by introducing the people in the room. 'Jack, this is Norman Waterman.' The Colonel indicated a fat man with a balding head, who stood up and shook Jack's hand. He had all the appearance of a politician, dressed in a brown suit with trousers that looked slightly too small around the waist. His face was round, and his jowls hung down like those of a bloodhound. 'He is our man from the Foreign Office. Next is Cameron Ferguson, our field operative in Africa; and, last but not least, is Corporal Herbert Duff.' The Corporal moved away from the window and nodded, giving Jack a better opportunity to see him. Although his appearance was scruffy, Jack sensed that he was SAS. 'Duffy to my friends!' he said.

Jack guessed that underneath all that stubble was a man hardly out of his teens. With shoulder-length blond hair he looked almost angelic. Ferguson, however, was a well-built man who, even from his seated position, Jack could see was tall. The Colonel resumed speaking.

'Cameron works for SIS. Now, I expect you're wondering what all this is about, and I think it would be better if I hand things over to Cameron.'

Cameron Ferguson stood up to his full height and walked to the front of the room. His eyes were steadfast, evaluating Jack.

'For your benefit, Jack, I shall tell you why we are all here. For some time now, MI6 has been monitoring a breakaway group of the Basque Separatist movement. This faction, that calls itself the Fist of Euskadi, has links with a man named Phillip Égalité.'

Ferguson moved to the projector as Herbert Duff closed the blinds. Looking towards the screen, Jack saw a photograph of a group of four people.

'This is Phillip Égalité. The man is a terrorist; a killer with an allegiance to no one except himself. We believed he was dead until three months ago when he turned up in Colombia where this photograph was taken.' Ferguson pointed to a man with a thin, grave face and a pencil moustache.

The Colonel noticed Jack's frown. 'Problem, Jack?'

Jack shook his head, scrutinising the picture. 'Where did you say this picture was taken?'

'In Colombia. Why?'

Jack hesitated, looking not at the man Égalité but a fifth person who was standing behind him, his face half concealed by shadow. 'That man in the background, the African chap. Who is he?'

'That's Samdi. We know little to nothing about him, only that he appeared when Égalité resurfaced.'

'Do you know him?' the Colonel asked, as Jack looked harder, his mind taken back to the jungles of Cameroon and the face of the tribal witch doctor hovering above him minutes after the attack.

Jack slowly shook his head. 'He reminds me of someone, but it can't be him.'

Ferguson looked irritated at the interruption and resumed his speech. 'Égalité was born in France, in a small village near the Pyrenees. His mother, Francine Égalité, was French and his father, Francisco Juan Aranaga, was Spanish. The young Égalité was educated in both France and Spain. We believe that he became involved with the Basque Separatists due to his father's views. Francisco Juan Aranaga was an active member of the Separatist movement, and the Égalités on the opposite side of the mountains were known to be wealthy sympathisers.'

Herbert Duff cut in. 'Isn't this a Spanish problem? I mean, where is our involvement—?'

Ferguson raised his hand. 'If you'll wait, I'm getting to that... Égalité majored in history, attained an honours degree in psychology and criminology and is a Master of Arts, specialising in ancient languages and cultures. He has a Masters in chemistry.'

'So he's highly educated?' Jack said.

Ferguson looked at Jack. 'To put it mildly; the man is a genius. Phillip Égalité shares the same surname as the citizen king of France, Louis Philippe Égalité, installed on the throne after the revolution, and has given himself the title of 'King Terrorist'. He thinks he's untouchable. His early beginnings were as an assassin. We can chalk up five international dignitaries who have fallen as his prey.

'Égalité was involved in terrorist activities as young as ten and joined the Foreign Legion when he was twenty-five. As I said, we believed him to be dead until our friends, the CIA, took this picture in Colombia. From what we have ascertained, he has been lying low somewhere in Africa.'

'You still haven't explained where the Fist of Euskadi comes into things,' Jack said, adding, 'or where the African connection is.'

'The first real hard evidence of the existence of the Fist of Euskadi was just over two years ago, when a bomb exploded in a shopping mall in Barcelona. The separatists denied any knowledge of the explosion. Later, the Fist of Euskadi claimed that the act had been committed on behalf of the people of Euskadi, meaning Basque country in Spanish.' Ferguson switched off the projector.

'In 1986, roughly two thousand pounds of weapons-grade uranium was stolen by a Russian nuclear scientist named Travinsky. The material was taken to secure him and his family a passage out of East Germany. Égalité operated as the intermediary for the Red Army Faction. An operation by the Russians recovered roughly one thousand pounds of uranium, which left another thousand pounds unaccounted for. Égalité was believed dead, and the missing uranium has not resurfaced.'

Ferguson directed everybody's attention to a second photograph on the screen. 'This man is Felix Grouper, a South African. Former member of the South African National Front movement. He's a nihilist, believing that all of society should be destroyed in order to build it anew on different principles. He studied nuclear science for four years at the Université Pierre et Marie Curie in Paris. The murder of a young girl caused Grouper to disappear, only to resurface with the French Foreign Legion in 1985. It was not until 1988 that Égalité became his commanding officer. However, Intelligence has since proved that Égalité and Grouper may have known each other at university. In 1981, Égalité was sitting his final year of a chemistry Masters degree at Pierre et Marie Curie. So it cannot be discounted. Grouper went AWOL in 1999. The men sent to retrieve him were all found dead. It is Grouper's knowledge of nuclear fission and Égalité's involvement with the missing uranium that leads us to believe that Égalité may be trying to construct a nuclear bomb.'

'To what purpose?' Jack asked.

'It appears that Égalité has been thriving on the sales of illegal arms.'

'He's going to sell it?' Jack asked.

'He would not be short of customers. But we want to prevent that from happening,' Norman Waterman added.

The Colonel took the chair. 'It seems that Égalité has made the Fist of Euskadi his mouthpiece. There has been talk of an auction. What exactly is under the hammer is a mystery, but there has been a lot of interest from a number of people worldwide. We also know that Égalité and Grouper have been hiding somewhere in Africa.' The Colonel addressed Duffy. 'Herbert has been working undercover in Ireland now for some time to convince O'Reilly to attend the auction.' Jack looked up as the projector was switched on again. 'And now I'll hand things over to you.'

Herbert Duff spoke from the back of the room. 'Shamus O'Reilly; staunch activist in the old IRA; believes that Sinn Fein have now gone soft by talking to the British. He wants a way to strike back at both the British and his fellow compatriots for their betrayal. He was once a friend of Gerry Adams, but, for obvious reasons, their friendship has now broken down. O'Reilly has a small following of around twenty men, but maintains links with his old, hardened buddies. At the moment he's doing a lot of talking, but I don't think it will be long before he makes a move of his own.'

Jack smiled. 'So, we use the IRA in a sting operation? Use a terrorist to catch a terrorist?'

'Exactly! And should O'Reilly survive, then he will no longer be a threat to us – he'll have a sentence hanging over his head,' the Colonel said.

Norman's hand moved to his collar as he unbuttoned the top of his shirt. 'As you probably know, the threat from terrorism is rising. Since 9/11, the days when the primary risk came from established groups with clear political aims have gone. Today their aims and objectives are more diffuse. Funding comes from the private sector, and terrorists no longer have to group together in order to conspire. They abuse technology, using modern communication systems to cross international boundaries. That is where you come in, Jack. We want you to infiltrate the Fist of Euskadi and locate the uranium. We want to know exactly what Égalité is up to.'

'Once you've done that, Jack,' the Colonel said, 'we will take over. We are going to give you a whole new identity. You are about to become the British Army's most wanted man. Your name is Jacob Portello.'

Another picture was flashed onto the projector. The man who appeared held an uncanny resemblance to Jack, making it a little clearer in Jack's own mind as to why he had been chosen for this mission. 'You were a captain in the Parachute Regiment's Path Finder Platoon, in charge of communications, with a flair for computers. What I mean to say is that you had a knack for hacking; it was discovered that you'd been selling vital information to the Real IRA. Imprisoned for treason, you served two years of a life sentence before you escaped, killing three soldiers.'

The Colonel paused, looking directly at Jack. 'Three days ago you hacked into SIS databases in an effort to erase your identity and downloaded sensitive information on Shamus O'Reilly and the Fist of Euskadi.' He held up a compact disk. 'This CD-ROM will be your bargaining chip. All of the information we have gathered on O'Reilly, Égalité and the activities of the Fist of Euskadi are contained on this disk. The real Captain Jacob Portello is dead. It was Herbert Duff who killed him on my orders.

'Portello's wife died in childbirth and he has no other living relatives, with the exception of the child. Jacob Portello was known to the Real IRA as Trooper. That is your code name for this mission.' The Colonel paused as another photograph was projected onto the screen. 'You will make contact with O'Reilly via Kerry O'Moore, a Second Lieutenant in the Army's Irish Guards. She has been working undercover with MI5 for the past five years. O'Reilly is her godfather, which is one of the reasons why MI5 recruited her. O'Reilly would know of Trooper, and hopefully this should lead you to your first contact. Providing that Herbert has been successful, that is.'

Norman Waterman stood up. 'Well, if that is all, gentlemen…' He glanced at his watch. 'I am expected back at the ministry in two hours.' Both he and Ferguson left the room, leaving the three soldiers together.

The Colonel retrieved four files from the desk. 'This is Jacob Portello's profile; make sure you familiarise yourself with it. Also, here is a file on Égalité, O'Reilly and Grouper. Watch yourself, Jack, around this one!'

Jack smiled. 'I always do, boss.'

'Oh, and one more thing. The woman, Kerry O'Moore – her code name is Scorpion.' He showed Jack a colour photograph of a woman with startling red hair and dazzling green eyes. 'This is her. She was your bit on the side when you were in Northern Ireland.'

A worried frown crossed Jack's brow. 'Won't she know that I'm not Portello?'

'She knows that you're not Portello because she knows that he's dead. It was her information that led to us discovering the true identity of Trooper!' The Colonel cast Duffy a glance. 'Could you leave us alone, please?' Duffy's eyes met Jack's as he passed.

Jack lit a cigarette, inhaling deeply on the smoke and releasing it slowly through his nose. He looked solemnly at the Colonel. 'I'm not expected back from this one, am I, boss?'

The Colonel clasped his hands before him on the desk. 'Do you remember the other day when I came to visit you? I said I was offering you something back.'

Jack nodded at the recollection.

'This is strictly off the record. But if you should find a way into this organisation, then what's to stop you from disappearing before the heat comes down?'

'Honour,' Jack said. 'You know that my honour won't allow me to do anything less than my best, even if it means my own life.'

The Colonel nodded in understanding. 'I was talking to your father the other day...' The Colonel observed Jack's jaw line tense.

'And how is the old man?' Jack enquired, his voice full of contempt.

'Haven't you two made up yet?'

'Should we?' It was a statement more than a question and the Colonel sensed the unresolved tension.

'He is your father.'

Jack began to laugh. 'Yes, and I'm his son, a chip off the old block – the brunt of his frustrations, you might say.'

The Colonel watched Jack through passive eyes. 'He knows the sort of man you are Jack. Of all people, you should be able to sympathise with him, if not understand him.'

Jack instinctively knew that what was being said was right, but Jack Hornsby Junior was a carbon copy of Jack Hornsby Senior.

Both were military men. Both had served in the most prestigious regiment in the world, and each was as obstinate as the other. 'How much does he know?' Jack asked.

'He knows that something big is going down, and he knows that I want you to be part of it, but as for details he doesn't—'

'You know, it was never over for him.' Jack broke in. 'He used to disappear for months at a time. He was never around. My brothers had all left home when he came back for good, and he seemed to be always battling inside himself. I suppose I brought a lot on myself, but it was the times when he was drunk...'

'You've been there, Jack. Surely you of all people would understand?'

Jack's face became straight and sullen. 'Oh, I understand, but it doesn't make it right!'

The Colonel rose from his seat and placed an affectionate hand on Jack's shoulder. 'All I can say is that he was asking about you. I'm going to give you ninety-six hours' leave. After which it will not be safe for you to walk around the streets.' Jack raised his eyebrows quizzically. 'The whole Trooper affair was a hush-hush operation. Officially, Jacob Portello is on the run. So when this comes out, it will be your face on every billboard and TV screen shortly after. So, I want you to report back here. What you do with the time is entirely up to you but, if you take my advice, then you will use it wisely.' Jack turned to leave the office. 'Oh, and Jack – think carefully about what I said earlier, about your father.'

His mind was made up; Jack would at least return home and see his mother, if no one else.

Left by himself, Jack sat down and studied the files. The profile on Jacob Portello was a standard résumé, detailing the career of the man. Educated at Cambridge, his psychological file stated that he was an under-achiever; that he could not aspire above his station; that he was a jealous individual who believed that things would, and should, come to him with little or no effort.

The report on Felix Grouper was not as mundane. As the grandson of a German officer in the SS, Grouper's Aryan blood was apparent in his genealogy. The picture that accompanied the document displayed a large man with an exceptional physique; his close-cropped blond hair gave the man a bullish, arrogant appearance.

The report also listed the man's preferences towards women. Felix Grouper's name appeared on Interpol's most-wanted list for the rape and murder of at least twelve women. These killings had been brutal and displayed Grouper's expertise with a blade.

Chapter 4

As the signs denoting Coventry loomed before him, Jack consoled himself with the fact that he was going back to his roots. He had conflicting feelings. He hadn't set foot in his home village of Hill Top for nine years. The last time he had returned was on his sister's second wedding to a banker. The man was named Tom and seemed a decent sort, but his father had held his own reservations about him.

The tension that had emerged between Jack and his father had been tangible throughout the service, and they had acted like two war veterans sizing each other up for one last battle. The other members of the family sensed the atmosphere, and Jack's mother did her utmost to keep her son and husband apart.

As Jack drove down the lane, trees crowded in on him from either side, the entrance to Templar's Hall stood on the right, back amongst the trees. The Knights Templar stronghold had been used as a school for over a hundred years. Then he saw Ash House standing at the top of the hill. A shudder ran through him: the building had about it an air of menace. It had a history, and murder had occurred there on more than one occasion. He remembered that the villagers used to say the house was haunted and called the place 'Devil House'.

He spotted his old homestead immediately; the estate he had lived on stood on the doorstep of the village. The front door was bright red and hadn't changed in thirty-odd years, although some modifications had been carried out on the house. Stone cladding lined the walls, and an extra room had been added to the attic. Pulling to the curb, Jack sat for a few moments in contemplation. He had no idea what sort of reception he was going to receive.

Climbing out of the car, he noticed a woman with a child stop outside number 68. 'I know you!' Jack said to her. Grabbing her round the waist, he laughed and said, 'All right kid!'

The woman jumped. Turning to face her assailant with a fury

in her eyes, her expression altered from anger to astonishment, as she viewed Jack with a quizzical expression.

'Has it been that long, Susan, that you don't recognise your baby brother?'

'Jack?' she said. 'Jack! My God, it is you!' She threw her arms around him, giving him a big squeeze. Susan was Jack's senior by five years, but Jack had always classed her as his kid sister because of her petite size.

'So how's it going?' he asked.

'Are you here for the funeral?' she replied. Jack frowned. 'Because if you are, you're late. It was an hour ago!' Jack's heart began to race; he was afraid to ask the question.

'Funeral? Who's died?'

'Uncle Tom! He died last Thursday. Dad's upset about it. They were very close.'

'I'm sorry,' Jack said. 'I liked Uncle Tom a lot.'

'And he was proud of you, though God knows why. He was always talking about you, saying you were a chip off the old block, the only one of us who followed in his and Dad's footsteps. He was always asking Dad about you.' Jack's mind was abruptly brought back into focus.

'And how is the old man?'

'Exactly that – old. He's changed, Jack. Changed an awful lot. He's not the same man that he was.'

Jack's concentration was turned away from his sister to the child. He squatted down, bringing his eyes level with the little boy's, who looked at him with big, puppy dog eyes. 'And who's this?'

'This is Jacky, my son.'

The little boy looked coyly from Jack to his mother. 'Say hello, then,' Susan said. 'This is your Uncle Jack!'

'Hello!' the boy said, as the front door to the house opened. Little Jacky ran inside, past an old and delicate-looking woman. Jack was dismayed; his mother looked a lot frailer than he remembered.

'Jack?' the old woman asked, her eyes filling with tears. Jack stood up straight as if he was on parade. All pride in him had been replaced with shame, the guilt of the absent years weighing heavy.

'Hello, Mum!'

Sarah Hornsby's face broke into a smile and she walked forward, grabbing her baby and hugging him tight. She snuffled, trying to hold back tears.

'Return of the prodigal son!' Jack said, feeling the joke went flat somewhere.

'Let me look at you!' Sarah said, dabbing at the tears that rolled down her cheeks with a handkerchief. Jack was stooped forward before her as she held both his cheeks between her wrinkled palms. 'Jack, my boy!' Her were eyes full of rapture as she reluctantly released him, trying to regain her composure. 'Look at me!' she said. 'A grown woman!'

Jack placed his hand on the side of her face. 'I'm sorry!' he said, his own eyes moist with emotion.

His mother turned. 'Come in, both of you!'

Jack moved aside, allowing his sister to enter first. Watching his mother's back, Jack felt both remorse and dishonour surge through him. There was brief laughter coming from the living room. A child's laughter was heard above all else, and then Jack heard his father's rigorous voice ride above all the others.

'Ah, here's little Jacky come to give his old grandpa a kiss and a hug!' Jack moved with anxiety, his stomach feeling leaden.

The living room was full of people, most of them family. Jack spotted his Aunt Jane standing alone with a glass of sherry. Looking at his father, Jack was shocked. Jack Hornsby Senior appeared worn, almost fragile, compared to the way Jack remembered him. He looked in Jack's direction with weary eyes, nodding his head as Jack entered. Jack immediately approached his aunt, offering his condolences.

Jack mingled with the people present. Most of them he knew, and the focal point of their attention was upon Jack Senior. Rising from his chair, the old man strode effortlessly forward with an outstretched hand.

Jack could see a respect in his father's eyes, as if all of the animosity between the two had melted away. Releasing his grip, Jack Senior returned to his armchair where his grandson jumped into his lap. Watching them both, Jack could see the pleasure the small child gave him.

As he approached his father, Jacky climbed off the old man's lap. 'I was sorry to hear about Uncle Tom,' said Jack.

'Damn fine man! You know, you remind me a lot of him.'

Jack smiled. 'Funny, he used to tell me that I reminded him of you!'

'Well, maybe you got a dose of us both!'

Jack saw regret in his dad's eyes. 'You miss him, don't you?'

'We went to hell and back together; fought the Jerry side by side. After the war, he returned home for our parents' sake. I remained, but I always was the headstrong one. He looked up to me! Never could work out why; we were practically the same age. Only ten months between us…' Jack Senior rose from his seat. 'Come with me, son?'

He made his way through the living room, past his relatives and friends, who were united in grief. Jack followed, pausing while a priest passed on words of condolence to his father. The old man nodded, shaking the priest's hand, before leading the way to his bedroom. He stooped down, pulling a large, wooden box out from underneath the bed. Jack was curious, watching as his father carefully raised the lid.

In the box was a sandy-coloured beret with the flamed sword pinned to it. Another box, containing a gun, was underneath, along with various pictures both in black and white and colour. As his father sorted through, he selected one, pulling out a velvet pouch containing a Victoria Cross.

'There were only ever two of them awarded during the Desert Rats' skirmishes with Rommel's Panzer divisions. One of them was awarded to your uncle. Do you remember when he used to recount a tale about saving my arse out in Algiers? Well, that story was perfectly true. Lieutenant David Stirling, the founder of the SAS, had sent us out on a recon. It was 31 August 1942 and Rommel was executing his attack on Alam Halfa. We ran into a rapidly advancing Panzer division. There was Tom, six others and myself. We had been spotted by the enemy and had to dig ourselves in. They had us pinned down from all angles. Two of our companions were mowed down by heavy gunfire and I caught one in the leg.'

Jack made to speak but his father carried on. 'We needed a

volunteer and Tom drew the short straw. It was a suicide mission – we all knew that – and a long shot at best. A one-man mission that would hopefully confuse Jerry into thinking they were being attacked from behind. In the confusion we were to hightail it back to base camp, report our findings and send in a squadron of bombers. But there would be no time to wait for Tom. If he survived, then he was to get back alone the best he could. We had no radio because it had been shot up, and we were alone against the might of the bloody German Army. Tom succeeded in his rear attack, taking out one of the tanks, which attracted the Desert Air Force Bombers. They demolished the Panzer division. It was only discovered later that it was on its way to back up Rommel's 15th and 21st Panzer Divisions in the assault on Alam Halfa. Monty defeated the Desert Fox, and we didn't find Tom until three days later. He was awarded the Victoria Cross for his valour. This is his medal. He gave it to me for safe keeping.' The old man looked at the medal. 'He never did ask me for it back. Later he told me that I deserved it more than he did, because I stayed with the regiment!'

Placing it back in the pouch, he offered it to Jack. 'It's yours now. You have continued what he and I started. Out of my five children – and I love them all in my own unique way – you are the one I'm most proud of.'

Jack was stuck for words. All his life he had tried to gain acceptance from his father, and now, at this time of remorse, his father was displaying to him what he had wanted most: his love. In his way, Jack realised that his father was trying to apologise.

'Anyway,' Jack said, taking a deep breath. 'How have you been keeping?'

Jack Senior lowered his gaze, suddenly becoming aware of the knot in his tie. 'I'm a survivor, Jack. You should know that. But not one word has there been from you in the last three years!' Jack lowered his head. 'I know we've had our problems, son… A lot of those were of my own making, but your mother…' He paused. 'She didn't deserve it!'

Jack felt all the shame of the lost years come crashing down on him in one swoop. He had to admit, at least to himself, that it was his own obstinate pride that had brought things to this.

His father spoke. 'I've been expecting you ever since Colonel

Windburn came to see me, asking about you. It seemed important that he find you, but I didn't know where you were. How could I, with no word? But from what I remember of that one, he was tenacious. Very headstrong.'

'That's right,' Jack agreed, and his father smiled.

'I knew he'd find you! So are you going to tell me what this is all about?'

Jack rebuked his father's question. 'You of all people shouldn't ask me that one!'

His father's face creased. 'But you're out of the army – unless...' He allowed his words to trail off as realisation dawned within him. 'The Colonel said to me he was working in information circles now, which can only mean one thing: Intelligence!' Jack couldn't help but smile. His dad might look old and frail, but his brain was as sharp as it ever was.

'Kind of, but I'll still be attached to the regiment.' He looked his dad straight in the eye. 'I'm going in deep, and I don't think I'll be returning. One way or the other, my life here's ended. They've given me a new identity. In just over seventy-eight hours, Jack Hornsby will never have existed. Whatever you see or hear, you don't know me!' Jack's father nodded his head in understanding.

'You will try to look after yourself, son, won't you?' Jack waved his arm at his side in the military signal for 'As you were'. His father gave a smile as Jack gave a thumbs up signal, meaning 'No enemy in sight or suspected'.

Returning downstairs to the family, Jack entered into a conversation with his mother and aunt. His brothers, sister and cousins all occasionally glanced in his direction; then Barry, Jack's eldest brother, approached them.

'We're off down the pub; things are getting a little too morose for me. Are you two coming, or what?' Jack looked out towards the front door where he could see his mother thanking people for coming before they left. Jack looked at his father, who was again seated in his armchair. Looking up, he gave the signal to advance.

The Bell Tavern had been a local to Jack since the age of fifteen. As he approached the door, memories began to flood back. When he entered, he was surprised at how much had changed. Though it retained a rustic charm, it appeared to be aimed at a younger generation. The interior had been changed, and steps now led down onto a dance floor.

It was early in the evening and the dance room accommodated a spattering of people of varying ages. Jack couldn't help but give a second glance to a group of girls who looked to be in their late teens. Walking up to the bar, Jack offered to buy the first round of drinks, ordering a triple whiskey and chaser for himself.

Knocking the whiskey straight back, he settled down with the pint sat before him, half listening to the conversation around him. The young girls whom he had seen at the bar were taking a particular interest in him.

Looking about the room, he tried to imagine it the way it used to be; his attention drawn towards the bar, he saw a woman studying him. She was slightly older than the girls on the dance floor; Jack estimated her to be in her mid-twenties. Her long deep-brown hair bordered on black and stretched the length of her back. Something about her caught Jack's eye, setting her apart from the other women in the room. Dressed in a pale blue suit, she looked refined.

Jack's preoccupation brought with it the impression that he knew her. There was something familiar about her face. As he sipped his pint, she disappeared, and Jack just caught the back of her as she left the bar. His focus began to waver, swimming in and out of convergence, like a mirage seen through a heat-scorched landscape. Jack was no longer in the tavern. He stood before Ash House at the top of the hill; the boy he had seen in Hereford standing in the open doorway. Behind him could be seen the House's victims, their bodies in various states of decay.

'Let's go round the back!' he heard somebody say. 'It's getting too noisy in here!' Jack blinked, and he was back in the Tavern, just as everybody rose from their seats and walked towards the rear of the pub. From what Jack remembered, this was where the bar was situated.

The bar area was considerably quieter than the dance room. Jack felt relief at leaving behind songs of Robbie Williams and Travis. He noticed the woman with long, dark hair perched on a bar stool, engaged in conversation with the barman.

Leaving his family to find seats, Jack wandered to the bar. He noted that the woman and barman took particular interest in him.

As he approached, he overheard the barman say, 'It is! As I live and breathe, it's Jack Hornsby!'

Jack allowed a quizzical expression to cross his face before recognition dawned upon him. The barman was a stout fellow with a bald head; the last time Jack had seen him he'd had a full head of hair.

'Paul? Paul Dempsey?' Jack enquired, as the man held his arms wide.

'It's been a long time, pal! About fifteen years!'

'What happened to you?' Jack said, shaking Paul's hand.

Paul self-consciously brushed his hand across the top of his head. 'This!' he said. 'One failed marriage and two kids!'

'Two kids?' Jack smiled.

'Two girls,' Paul replied. 'I bet you don't remember my kid sister, Lisa, do you?' The niggling feeling that Jack had felt earlier was suddenly answered. He did know the woman. She was some five years his junior, and he remembered her as a little girl with pigtails, who had always annoyed him when they had been younger. He also remembered that same girl giving him a kiss just before he'd left for the army.

Now that same girl stood before him, all grown up and certainly not a child any more. 'The one that got away!' she declared, in a sweet but dusky voice.

'Lisa?' Jack smiled. 'The same Lisa who was always making a nuisance of herself when we were kids? The same Lisa who was a bit of a tomboy?'

Lisa glanced into her drink. 'All grown up now, Jack! As are you!' Her eyes were suggestive as she studied him from the rim of her glass.

Paul was carrying on a conversation, but Jack had lost the thread. Lisa fascinated him for reasons he could not fathom. In a moment when he thought she wasn't looking, he feasted his eyes over the rest of her appearance. The suit she wore was of fine quality and embraced her body, accentuating her curves.

Barry approached the bar, nodding in Paul's direction. 'If I could borrow my kid brother back, it's not very often he comes home! Anyway, you've got a pub to run, and your first duty is to serve me!' Paul began to laugh, moving to one of the hand pumps.

'Your usual, is it, Barry?'

'Yep, and whatever my brother here's having and…' He reeled off the rest of his order. Jack turned his attention back to Lisa.

'Will you join us?' he asked. Lisa gave the table behind a brief glance; she spotted Jack's sister as the lone female sitting with a group of men.

'It looks like Susan needs rescuing!' Lisa smiled, and Jack gazed deeply into her eyes, becoming momentarily lost. They were startling, kindled by hidden fires that gave the warmth of burnished amber stones.

Jack leant over the bar, speaking to Paul. 'Who would have thought that the scrawny little girl with the pigtails would have bloomed into such a flower?' Paul grinned, as if the compliment had been passed to him. Lisa blushed.

'I think we had better move; your family seem a little lost without you!' Lisa said. Aware that he had embarrassed her, he instantly regretted it. He was no longer that young soldier out on the pull on a Friday night. There was something loving in this woman, and, despite every effort to conceal it, this single aspect of her persona shone through.

'Hello, Susan!' Lisa said, as she approached the table. 'Would you mind if I joined you?'

Susan smiled. 'Not at all, Lisa. As you can see, I'm surrounded by a bunch of Neanderthals. Well, nearly all, anyway!' Susan looked directly at Jack.

'I'm flattered that you don't hold me in the same high regard as you do the rest of my brethren!' Jack retorted.

Susan began to laugh and Lisa joined her.

Seating himself between his sister and Lisa, Jack stretched both his arms out along the back of the seat. 'What more could a man want?' he said. 'To come home to two such beautiful and remarkable women!' Lisa turned to him, smiling coyly.

'And did they teach you to be so smooth with your tongue in the army then, Jack?'

'No, that's something I taught myself!' They all started laughing. 'So, Lisa, what is it that you do – I mean as regards work?'

'I used to work for a solicitors' as a legal executive; my boyfriend and boss wasn't a very nice man!'

'What do you mean?' Jack queried.

'He used to like using his fists! Now I'm working for a charitable group called Food for Africa. The money's not great – well, it's pretty poor actually – but I get to travel. Next week I'm flying out to Africa.'

It was like someone had just dug up Jack's grave. Everything and everybody in the room suddenly ceased to exist, and standing next to the bar was the boy that had died in Jack's arms, calling to him. 'Join me! Join me, Jack!'

Jack was thrown out of his nightmare as quickly as he had entered it. He was back in the bar; the humdrum of a multitude of conversations buzzed in his head. 'Jack! Jack! Are you all right?' It was Lisa who spoke, and Susan had hold of his arm.

'I'm all right!' he said, trying to dispel the after-effects of his latest experience.

'Was it something I said?' Lisa enquired. 'You went all spaced out when I mentioned Africa.'

'Africa is a big place. Where in Africa are you going?' Jack asked, taking the top off his pint. Lisa slid closer to him.

'Niger. Have you been there?'

Jack nodded his head. 'I was stationed there for a while.'

Lisa's eyes began to sparkle with interest. 'Tell me about it; is it really as romantic as I've heard?'

'I wouldn't go that far. It's a very wild and dangerous place, but it is very beautiful. It's nature at its finest. What Africa needs most is educating. Already they are beginning to destroy their heritage – killing the animals, the elephants and the rhinos – and the people who could stop it, who *should* stop it, are the people who are instigating it!'

When Jack looked at Lisa, her elbows were propped on the table, her chin resting in her hands.

'I bet you have some tales to tell!' The comment hit a raw nerve. Jack looked away sharply.

'Do you know that my brother now owns this place?'

Jack was glad of the change in conversation. 'He owns the pub?' Jack looked round, noticing that all his family had gone. Paul was busy collecting the empty glasses off the tables and overheard his sister's comment.

'What, you didn't know?' He beamed at Jack, who could see the pride in his face. 'All mine!' Paul said. 'Lock, stock and barrel!' Paul sat down, launching himself into a long-winded account of how he came by the pub and the prices of the best ales.

Jack found his mind wandering to Ash House and the boy. 'Do people still live in the big house on the hill?' he asked.

Paul stopped short. 'The bloody place should be pulled down! As if it doesn't have a jaded enough past as it is! Of course, you wouldn't know. Twelve years ago, they caught a woman eating the remains of her husband. Her name was Barbara Blyth. She and her husband seemed a decent enough sort: turned it into an old people's home. There was a series of articles about her and Devil House in *The Telegraph* for over six months. Now some idiot millionaire has bought it and is going to turn it into an old people's home – again! As if it hasn't been that before! The place is jinxed: no good has come to anyone who has gone up there.'

Jack remembered going into the house once on a dare, when he had felt something touch him. 'Ghost stories!' Jack laughed, feeling that his humour was a little too hollow.

Later, as he walked Lisa home, Jack mused on how well Paul had done for himself. Lisa agreed, telling him a bit about Paul's first wife and their consequent break up. 'It took him a long time after the break up of his first marriage to accept things. I helped in my own way by loaning him a bit of capital so he could buy himself into the pub business. He began to remember his youth, and you in particular. When the Tavern went on the market, he had to have it, saying that Jack and he used to have some wicked laughs in there. You know, he never really was the same after you left. He thought you'd be mates for ever!'

Jack smiled, remembering the things they had got up to as kids. 'He was like my brother. "The terrible twins" they used to call us at school!'

'I remember. My mum used to think you were a bad influence!'

'Me?' Jack feigned being hurt. 'Well, maybe I did lead him on a little!'

Lisa brought them to a standstill outside a quaint little semi. Jack had no idea of how far they had walked, or even where he was, but glancing behind him he could see Ash House perched on its eyrie, overlooking the whole village.

'Well, this is where I live!' she said. 'You coming in, or are you going to stand there all night?' Jack was a little stuck for words at her brash statement. 'Don't worry, this is not something I do on a regular basis.' She inserted the key in the lock and entered the house. It took Jack a few seconds to decide to follow her in.

Sitting on the sofa, Jack curiously examined the room; it was very warm and inviting. The walls were a subtle peach colour, and, when the lights were turned low, they gave a sense of serenity. Two pictures hung on the wall. The first comprised wavy blue lines: it reminded Jack of the water sign for Aquarius. It wasn't flamboyant, like a lot of modern art, but then it wasn't Jack's idea of art really. The second painting, however, was of a scene. Mountains stood as a backdrop to green pastures with a brook running through a meadow. Jack could even see a red squirrel finely etched, sitting in a tree. This was the kind of art that Jack appreciated. He was no connoisseur, but he did know what he liked.

Lisa appeared in the doorway wearing a black negligée. 'This is not what I expected!' Jack said.

Lisa gave a half smile and turned away. 'Are you turning me down?'

'I'm not saying that!' he said, as she turned to face him, looking sad. 'I'm leaving shortly, and frankly I don't know if I'm coming back. There's little here for me any more.'

Lisa sat down next to him, crossing her legs, satisfied in the knowledge that Jack was enjoying the spectacle. 'I'm not usually this forward, you know!' she whispered in his ear, and tenderly brushed her lips against his. She took a sharp intake of breath. 'You're cold! Never for one moment…' she said between kisses, 'did… I… think… I… would… be… doing… this!'

Her face held close to Jack's, she looked deeply into his eyes, seeing a hardness and sorrow. Pressing herself to him, she said. 'Jack Hornsby…' She began to pop the buttons of his shirt. 'How long's it been?' Her hand explored beyond the fabric of his shirt, running down, caressing his pectorals, feeling hardened scar tissue.

He tensed. 'Too long!' he replied, slipping his hand into the small of her back. Her legs coiled around his waist as he stood up and headed for the stairs. Their mouths opened, entwined in a kiss.

Removing his clothes, he moved close to her. He felt a burning desire unlike anything he had felt before. Tasting her lips with his tongue, he detected a slight wisp of aniseed from the Pernod she had been drinking earlier.

Jack kissed her without the ferocity of their earlier endeavour. Gently caressing her neck with his mouth, he ventured lower to her breasts, perfect orbs that heaved with the soft rise of her breathing. Their lovemaking was intense and sensuous, until at length they lingered in each other's caress.

Rolling onto his back, Jack stared up through the darkness at the ceiling. He was shaking his head. 'It's never been like this before!' He spoke to the darkness, looking for answers in its inky depths, hearing Lisa sigh beside him.

'You can't imagine what it did for me!' She leaned over and kissed the tip of his nose. 'You know, Jack, I could learn to love somebody like you!' She felt him smiling in the darkness.

'I know I could love someone like you!' Turning over he pulled her so that she was straddled on top of him. 'OK!' he said. 'Now it's your turn!' Lisa giggled.

When morning came, Jack was reluctant to leave; he tried to think of all the reasons he shouldn't go. For the first time, he had felt wanted, with a family and a special person with whom he could spend the remainder of his life. He didn't expect to see Lisa again and felt guilty.

Chapter 5

When Jack returned to Hereford, he met the Colonel along with another man. Jack sensed that there was a reason for this meeting.

'This is Captain Graham Harrington,' the Colonel said. 'After you locate the whereabouts of the stolen uranium, Graham will be in charge of the operation to recover it.' Harrington stepped forward to shake Jack's hand.

'I don't know how much you know about radioactive material, but it's safe to say that you know to keep well clear of it. The uranium is weapons-grade, from what we can ascertain from Russian intelligence: ninety to ninety-five percent of the isotope 235. That means a chunk roughly the size of a coffee mug, with conventional explosives placed around it, would have the equivalent explosive power of the Hiroshima bomb! Jack – no heroics when you locate the material: hand things over to us. My team has had special training in this sort of thing.'

Jack nodded his agreement. 'You'll get no argument out of me! My cover is watertight then?' he asked the Colonel.

'It has to be. You are our wild card. Égalité is a highly dangerous individual. Could you imagine what would happen if a nuclear weapon were to fall into the hands of terrorist organisations? Governments would fall and chaos reign. We don't know if he is selling the material on its own or with some kind of device. That's what we want you to find out. We do know that Felix Grouper is a silent partner in a hotel in Niger. This is where we think he and Égalité have been hiding.' Jack found himself thinking about Felix Grouper and his nihilistic ideals.

'There's just one other thing, boss. When do I go?'

As Jack sat on flight 334 headed for Belfast, he thought about the task he had been given. His job: to infiltrate a known terrorist organization, the IRA, as a means to infiltrate another. All documentation appertaining to Jack Hornsby Junior had effectively been erased, meaning that he no longer existed. Now he had to become another man, adopt another identity to complete his mission.

The aircraft shuddered; Jack felt his stomach lurch as the plane abruptly dropped. A metallic voice came over the speaker system and spoke calmly in a reassuring manner. 'Hello, ladies and gentlemen. There is no need to be alarmed, as we've just passed…'

The words faded into insignificance as Jack turned and saw the boy sitting beside him. He was about to speak, when his eyes opened to see an air stewardess bending over him. She smiled reassuringly. 'Could you put your seat belt on, sir? We are going to land shortly.' Thanking the stewardess politely, he did as she instructed.

Jack disembarked to be greeted by cold drizzle. It's nice to be back, he thought. He carried with him a briefcase containing the CD-ROM.

He began to look at faces. He'd been told that Second Lieutenant Kerry O'Moore would meet him on arrival, and he had her face firmly etched into his mind. Spotting her standing by the entrance to the departures lounge, Jack assumed she had been briefed as he had.

She waved at Jack's approach, looking him up and down. Running her tongue across the top of her teeth, she said, 'Hello, lover!' in a deep and heavily accented voice. Throwing her arms around him, she embraced him like a long-lost love.

When their lips parted, the woman began to giggle. Hugging him again tightly, she whispered in his ear, 'Follow me, and smile! You look like someone who has just escaped from the Maze!'

Second Lieutenant Kerry O'Moore or Scorpion, as she was better known in intelligence circles, tossed her head, giving her long and vibrant red hair buoyancy, compelling it to dance across her shoulders. Smiling amiably, Jack waited for a more opportune moment. Getting clear of the crowd, he roughly grabbed her by the arm, pulling her to one side. 'The stars were bright the first time we met!' Jack spoke with a voice that contained sceptical undertones.

'The sun is hot for the time of year,' she said, casting him an acrimonious look, and wrenched herself away. Walking close together, they left the airport.

They crossed the car park to a battered Morris Minor and Kerry threw open the driver's door and climbed in. Jack did likewise on the opposite side. Once inside the car, Kerry asked abruptly, 'What the hell do you think you were doing?' Her eyes challenged him.

Jack remained impassive. 'I thought you would identify yourself by giving me a phrase.' Jack nestled a small-calibre gun in his lap. He pointed it directly at Kerry. Kerry glanced at the gun, her face not flinching one inch. 'You failed!' Jack stated, categorically.

'Before you pull that trigger and possibly make the biggest mistake of your life, answer me one question. Have you ever been to Ireland before?'

'Once or twice,' Jack replied, his hand still firmly grasping the gun.

'Fucking great!' Kerry stated. 'They've sent me a squaddie!' Jack's eyes diminished to scant pinpoints as Kerry haughtily continued. 'In the middle of the airport, when the skies look like they are about to open up, my saying a stupid thing like "the sun is hot for the time of year" would have sounded a bit strange, don't you think?'

Jack had to admit that the code phrase was not the most original and, if it had been left to him, he would have used something more appropriate; but delivering himself into the lion's jaws was not on his agenda either. He relaxed his trigger finger slightly, but he did not remove the gun from sight. His eyes were unwavering as he spoke. 'Of course I've been to Ireland before, which is why I am acting like I am. It's my arse on the line, not yours! And I'm not one hundred percent sure you are who you're claiming to be!'

'What do you want me to do? Give you my life history? And it's not just your arse on the line, it's mine as well. I'm the plant, remember?' Kerry replied, scorn evident in her voice. 'So what else do you want to know? That my code name is Scorpion? That I'm a Second Lieutenant in the Irish Guards working in liaison with MI5? That my mother was English and my father Irish? That I spent the first fourteen years of my life in Ireland before my father killed my mother? That I was raised in England by my grandparents?'

Jack held up his hand; he had heard enough. The information Kerry had relayed to him he had committed to memory.

'I'm sorry,' he said, 'but you can't be too careful.'

'Too right you can't!'

Jack saw the anger in the woman's eyes. Her face was stern, finely etched and Jack mused on how dazzlingly attractive she looked. 'The reason why I did what I did is because I think I'm being tailed.'

Jack scanned the car park without making it obvious. He couldn't help feeling that he might have compromised the entire operation.

'Don't worry, Jack. Our dramatics will only have strengthened our case. Ours is meant to be a love-hate relationship; anyone observing would have assumed it was a tiff. But,' she said, 'I don't like guns being pointed at me.'

Silence filled the car, then Kerry said, 'OK, we haven't got off to the greatest of starts here, so I suggest we start again.'

Jack observed that she had calmed herself down considerably. Kerry started the engine and drove out of the car park.

'Where are we going?' Jack asked.

'Back to my place.'

Jack settled back in his seat, attempting to enjoy some of the world's most beautiful countryside, but his mind was overwrought, focused on the job at hand. He was in enemy territory, and caution was of the utmost importance. He checked the side mirror again to ensure they had picked up no tails. All seemed quiet, though Kerry's eyes never left the road, her jawline set in a stern resolve. She spoke, observing Jack out of the corner of her eye.

'You say you've been to Ireland before?'

'I've done my stint,' he replied, as Kerry casually glanced across at him, noticing a faint scar that ran down his left temple.

'Battle scars, hey?' She smiled, returning her attention to the road. 'So, what's your name – besides Jacob, I mean?' Jack remained silent. 'Silent type? Jacob was the silent type and a ruthless bastard! Are you ruthless?'

'Jack. Call me Jack. And I've been known to be, on occasion.'

Kerry smiled. 'Convenient. I used to call Jacob, Jack. It was a sort of pet name. Always thought Jacob was too righteous for him.'

An uneasy silence descended within the confines of the car, forcing Kerry to continue the one-sided conversation. 'Don't be fooled by this supposed peace process.'

Jack looked at her. 'I'm not.'

'Things are not always as they seem, particularly here. This time of peace is a sham. The South is still plotting against the North.' Jack grunted an agreement as Kerry persisted in her coaxing. 'You're a quiet one, Jack.'

'I'm a man on the run. I'm wanted for half a dozen murders.'

'But we're supposed to be old lovers!'

Jack gave a quaint smile. 'So, you want me to fuck you?' The acrimony was evident in his voice.

'I didn't say that!' Kerry protested, offended by Jack's words. 'We are supposed to be posing as a couple, so you need to lighten up a little.' She turned her head away from him. 'I don't want it to look like I'm here under duress.'

Jack frowned, questions forming in his mind. 'Are you?'

The question was point blank. Kerry's face flared, showing some of her earlier fiery temper.

'Like you, I'm doing my job!' Her voice was deep with an Irish tone, rich and melodic, that gave it a husky touch, but Jack detected a slight waver in her accent. It wasn't noticeable to the untrained ear, but Jack had enough experience behind him to distinguish certain abnormalities. His life had depended on it once. As it did now.

'Your accent's wavering,' Jack said. Kerry smiled, realising that he had seen through her pretence.

'Why, aren't you the perceptive one, Jack,' she said dropping the accent altogether.

'I take it that you're not entirely in agreement with your orders?' Jack probed.

'I'm not very happy with the fact that I might be involved in something that will destroy the peace process altogether. I've worked long and hard to get myself where I am now, and I'm not happy about the prospect of becoming a target if something should go wrong!'

'Don't worry yourself unnecessarily. I'm not interested in the Provisional IRA, the Real IRA or the New IRA. I was told that you would introduce me to Shamus O'Reilly.' Jack observed Kerry's eyes widen, and she became a little tense.

'I was told none of this,' she stated. 'I was instructed that I should accommodate you, and introduce you to one or two of the old Provisional's larger cogs.'

'Isn't O'Reilly one of those inner mechanisms?' In Jack's mind, he was still not at ease with this redhead.

'Yes, but…'

'There you have it then!'

'O'Reilly is a loose cannon. He is disgusted that Sinn Fein is having anything to do with the British Government, and he thinks the Real IRA, as they are calling themselves, are nothing but a joke. He believes that the IRA has gone soft and the cause is over, which is why he's been hanging around some foreigners.'

'Foreigners?' Jack queried.

'Yes; I've seen him with a bunch of what I'd call rough necks. These people look like the types that you don't mess with: military types that have seen too much action. To be honest, they scare me!'

'How long have you been involved with Intelligence?' Jack asked.

'I was in the Women's Royal Army Corps attached to the Irish Guards for five years. I was approached by a major, who told me I was the ideal candidate for special duties. It turned out that he was part of an MI5 recruitment drive. You see, my mother was English Catholic and while in England met a dashing Irishman. They courted and later married, moving to Ireland. My mother died at my father's hand, and he took over my upbringing. That was, until he tried to blow up a British patrol. He was killed when the bomb blew him up as well. I found myself being passed around the Irish social services for a while, before my grandparents claimed me on my mother's side. I was taken back to England and raised there.'

Jack saw a checkpoint ahead of them and felt his stomach

clench in a tight knot. This part of the plan hadn't been thought out very well. If they were stopped and searched, Jack knew that the game would be up before it had begun. When they brought the car to a standstill, two armed men approached both sides of the car. 'Don't say a word,' Kerry said. 'Let me do all the talking.'

The Ballymurphy estate in West Belfast was a staunch IRA and Sinn Fein stronghold, and on numerous occasions in the past had been the focal point of much of the sectarian troubles. This was a place known as dead man's land if you were not a Provisional supporter. The walls of the estate were daubed with graffiti, some filling entire walls of end-terrace houses, depicting men wearing balaclavas and holding guns. This graffiti alone marked the boundaries of the territory and acted as a deterrent to any wayward traveller.

Kerry turned right into a road and stopped the car. Jack's eyes were vigilant, his senses as keen as ever. In this part of Northern Ireland, Jack felt unsafe; it was like hostile eyes were watching from dark windows. All seemed quiet, but in this area it was best to be on your guard, especially as he knew the enemy would know that he was coming. The street was deserted, but that gave Jack little comfort.

Climbing out of the car, he scrutinised for anything out of the ordinary. Kerry had approached the door of a mid-terraced house and held the door wide open. The slight drizzle that had welcomed Jack from the plane at the airport had turned into a downpour. Jack ran from the car under the rain-swept sky.

Darkness crept across the grey sky. Jack entered the house as Kerry flicked a switch. 'You'd better get out of those wet things,' she suggested, roughly towelling her own hair with a pink towel. 'If you want to freshen up, then there are fresh towels in the cupboard in the bathroom.' She turned on the landing light. Jack nodded, ascending the stairs.

Jack welcomed the steamy caress of the shower. As the hot water ran down his body, it both cleansed and invigorated him.

Above the splatter of water, Jack heard Kerry's voice. He had neglected to pull the shower curtain across, and when he washed the soap from his eyes he was confronted by Kerry. She wore a smile on her lips as she appraised his toned muscle. Seeing the scar on his chest, she winced, noticing a purple, marbling effect on his right side. She turned away, embarrassed, when she realised that Jack was looking at her.

Casually, he pulled the curtain completely across, depriving her of any further view. Asking for a towel, he stepped out of the cubicle.

Kerry wore a light blue bathrobe, and her partially dried hair hung lank around her face in a wild tangle. She smiled in a knowing way, stepping past Jack. 'Thank you!' she said, allowing the robe to fall to the floor. Jack caught a glimpse of lily-white skin and smiled at the subtle yet direct way in which she did this.

'What do I do for clothes?' Jack called back, hearing the spray of the shower as the water was turned on.

'There's another robe in the bedroom! It used to be Jacob's!'

Locating it hanging behind the door, he shrugged it on, wandering to the window and gazing out onto the rain-swept street below. A line of street lamps lit the road with amber radiance that shone off the wet tarmac. He watched two people walk past with the hoods of their raincoats pulled tightly around their heads and wondered if it was a genuine guard against the weather or a shield against suspecting eyes.

Jack glimpsed Kerry's reflection framed in the open doorway behind him. 'It must be very lonely having to live and operate here in the heart of a war zone,' he said to the window pane.

She looked at her feet. 'It isn't that hard: it's part of what I have to do.'

'But aren't you scared? I mean – and don't take this the wrong way – but you're a woman, alone, here in this dreadful place. You know what they would do to you if they found out?' Jack didn't wait for a reply. 'I do! I've seen it. And the women get it worse than the men.'

'Of course I'm scared, but dead is dead, Jack, no matter what was done beforehand. The result would be the same for anybody crossing the IRA. I play the game in the hope that it will bring an end to the violence. I take my comfort when and where I can.'

Jack turned around and saw she was naked, the soft swell of her breasts heaving as she breathed a little fast. Jack felt himself stir – this woman was beautiful. As she looked into his eyes, Jack was compelled to pull her to him, his hand cupping her breast as he kissed her.

Lying in bed, Kerry asked, 'Is there anyone back home? A wife? A girlfriend?' When Jack declined to answer, Kerry laughed. 'There is, isn't there? You're married?'

Jack shook his head. 'No, I'm not married. Maybe I should be, but I've never allowed anyone to get that close…until recently.' Kerry felt remorse flood through her, thinking that there was no reason why this time should be any different – all the men in her life had left her one way or another.

'Tell me about her.'

Jack remained silent. If he escaped from this job, he now knew that there could be a life waiting for him, but Kerry prompted. 'You love her don't you?'

Jack gave a wry laugh, and answered a question with a question. 'What is love?' he asked. 'Love is passion! We have just experienced passion. Does that mean that we love each other?'

Kerry remained silent, tears beginning to well in her eyes. Jack felt her suffering.

'I'm sorry!' he said. 'If I've upset you, then I apologise.'

Kerry adopted a stern resolve, hardening herself as she had before. Men had come and men had gone; it was part of the job. She couldn't keep on doing this to herself, but this time she felt different. This strange enigma, this unusual man beckoned without realising he was doing so. By now, Kerry had realised that there were no knights in shining armour, no men with white hats who might come riding in to sweep her off her feet; but Jack – if that really was his name – had a power about him, a strong resolve that drew her like a star to a black hole.

'I take it, then, that there is no one special in your life?' Jack asked.

Kerry gave a derisive laugh. 'There are men, men who would dearly love to be where you are tonight. But they're not the right men!'

Jack reasoned that it would be pointless moving the conversation any further. Rolling onto his side, he guiltily thought of Lisa.

They were both violently roused out of their sleep by a crashing and banging. The noise came from the front door. Kerry's arms held him and she hugged up close, as the pounding came again. Not very professional, Jack thought. He knew it was trouble, but professionals, even Provos, would have gained entry without kicking up so much of an advertisement.

'Hadn't you better answer that?' Jack said, feeling Kerry's reluctance to do so. 'They obviously know we're in here!'

Kerry hesitantly climbed out of bed. Jack listened as she descended the stairs. Reaching down underneath the bed, he grasped the handle of a Browning. There was a muffled conversation at the door, followed by a squeal from Kerry.

Jack positioned himself beside the door, his gun held at the ready as heavy feet began to climb the stairs. He reasoned there were two of them, and he prepared his offence accordingly.

The door was thrown wide, and Jack had just enough time to see the gun push through, before he rammed the door back with force, trapping the wrist of the would-be assailant. The weapon dropped, and was followed by a loud curse as Jack rolled forward, collecting the discarded weapon. He lay on his back, both guns held at arm's length before him.

The door was kicked wide again, this time crashing harmlessly into the bedroom wall. There, standing in the doorway, was a thickset man with a heavy growth of beard; he was nursing his wrist. Behind him was a second man, with a gun directly pointed at Jack's prone form.

'Move and you're dead!' the thin man hollered, but there was little persuasion or confidence in his voice. He looked uncertain, and Jack could see consternation in his eyes. Jack's old man once told him that if you ever showed the enemy fear, they would feed off it and play it to their own advantage.

Now Jack placed a relaxed expression on his face. Smiling in a knowing way, his mouth formed a sneer. 'From this distance I could take both of you out with a single shot!'

'Not if we shoot ye in the head first,' the bearded man said.

Jack smiled, maintaining his façade. 'Don't overrate head shots,' he said. 'Too many unpredictable vectors. The skull is the hardest part of the body – it's virtually armour-plated! If the bullet doesn't strike right, then it skims right off. I'd be unconscious but alive. Whereas you two will be dead, because I aim for the heart!'

He allowed the two Irishmen to ponder what had been said. Looking confused, both men momentarily glanced at each other for assurance. The wiry man holding the gun stepped forward, his weapon still trained on Jack's prone position. 'You've got a bloody cheek coming here,' he scorned.

'Oh, and why is that?' Jack's eyes were locked on his would-be assassin, his muscles poised for the slightest hint of aggression.

'We know who you are!'

'And who am I?' Jack asked, bringing sarcasm into his voice.

The bearded man with the injured wrist began to speak. His eyes were beady and full of hatred. 'A bloody British soldier! And a fucking Para at that!' The contempt in his voice was almost tangible, and he spoke words that were laced with disgust. 'We'll be seeing you around!' The two men began to back away. 'Or then again, maybe we won't!' he added, mimicking a gun with his thumb and forefinger. Jack smiled, his gun hands never wavering from the retreating targets. As they went, he heard one of them say, 'Traitorous bitch!'

When the men had gone, Kerry appeared in the doorway. Her bathrobe was torn and a red welt was beginning to swell around her left eye. She was crying, and she tried to pull the torn robe around her like a shield. Her eyes were wide with fear, and she was shaking.

'Anyone you know?' Jack asked, seeing the condition Kerry was in. With fresh bouts of tears threatening to overwhelm her, Kerry rushed forward to Jack, who enfolded her in his arms. 'Who were they? O'Reilly's mob?'

'No. O'Reilly is opposed to the peace process, but basically he knows that as far as the political aspect goes it's a done deal. The two men you just met are brothers – Bob and Ted Murphy.'

Between sobs, Kerry told him about the two brothers who were becoming an increasing presence on the estate.

'They're small-time hoods! At the moment they're being left alone, but words have been uttered that maybe it's time to quiet them down a bit. They claim to have links to the Real IRA, but this is unsubstantiated, and it's believed that they're using this to increase their standing.'

'Can they be called off?'

'No. If they know you are here, then so will everybody else. Word travels fast around here. I wouldn't be surprised if they hadn't been put up to it. I'm frightened, Jack. We've got to get out of here and quick!'

Jack agreed – it wasn't just his arse he had to look after now. Kerry was his main concern: she was in danger. Jack was not the type of man to leave a comrade behind. If he had been alone, then he would have found a place to lie low for a few days and wait things out. 'We're going to have to meet O'Reilly pronto,' he said.

Kerry appeared to be unnerved by the suggestion and hesitated to answer. 'Word's out, Jack! I was going to arrange the meeting tomorrow, but now my name's going to be mud – I don't even want to think about the repercussions – and O'Reilly's not due back until next week!'

Jack thought for a moment, running the remaining available options through his mind.

'Do you know where O'Reilly is?' he asked.

'He's south.'

'But do you know where?'

Kerry nodded her head, fresh tears beginning to well in her eyes. Jack had to improvise.

'Have you anywhere else we can stay?'

Kerry nodded, looking at him in bewilderment. 'Just south of the border. My father owned a small cottage there.'

'Then that's where we will go!'

Chapter 6

Daylight had just begun to trace its way across the heavens; the rain had stopped, but the sky looked oppressive. Jack gave Kerry no time to pack; he ushered her into the car, climbing into the driving seat.

Kerry directed him, though Jack made many turns and double backs to throw off any tail, crossing the border into Southern Ireland. The contrast was stark. Where the North sported housing estates and concrete jungles, the South lay open to sprawling fields and woodland. They drove for a further twenty minutes before Kerry instructed him to turn into a grove of trees. The lane wound its way to a quaint cottage with a thatched roof that was reminiscent of fairy stories. A brick-built well lay to the left, and the garden was surrounded by a picket fence that was almost hidden by weeds.

The door to the cottage was sheltered by a thatched porch. As they walked up the garden path, Jack mused on how picturesque it looked. 'My dad used to tell me a leprechaun lived at the bottom of the well!' Kerry said, smiling, as she reached in her bag and produced a set of keys.

'Did he grant you any wishes?'

'No, but I remember searching for his pot of gold when I was little!' Jack laughed as Kerry inserted the key in the lock.

When the door opened, they were greeted by a musty smell. It had been some time since the house had last been used. The front door opened into the main living area; a door led off at the back, leading to the kitchen. The stairs wound their way into the attic.

'It's an outside toilet, I'm afraid. There's not many luxuries here!'

'I've lived in worse,' Jack said, thinking of all the cramped static observation posts he had found himself living in for days, even weeks at a time.

The furniture in the cottage was covered with dust sheets, and

Jack had to stoop slightly in order to enter. 'How many people know about this place?'

'Just O'Reilly. He and my father used to use it as a hide in times of trouble.'

'So O'Reilly is not just an acquaintance of yours?' Jack asked, maintaining ignorance.

Kerry flashed him a reproachful look. 'No, actually he's my godfather!' Kerry removed the dust covers from the furniture. 'We can't stay here for ever! It's only a matter of time before someone realises.'

'You worry too much. We've just got to get to O'Reilly before anyone else does.'

'If he suspects me, then I'm dead as well as you!'

'Trust me,' Jack said. 'Where is O'Reilly?'

Kerry stared at Jack, a loose lock of her red hair falling forward to cover her eye. 'I don't know where he is now, but I do know where he will be in about seven hours from now. He'll be in the Wailing Banshee; it's a pub ten miles from here.'

Jack told Kerry to get some rest before they left. Kerry curled herself up on the sofa, falling asleep. As Jack watched her sleep, he thought she looked so vulnerable and wondered why she willingly put herself in danger.

A noise alerted him. Checking his Browning and the weapon he had acquired from the Murphy brothers was loaded, he quietly crept from the house. Skirting the perimeter of the cottage, he found nothing out of place. When he decided to check the car, Jack spotted someone standing in the tree line in front of him.

The figure was small, that of a child and, as he approached, the child turned and Jack recoiled, almost firing his gun. Standing before him was the native boy that had been haunting him. His body was decomposed, and Jack could smell the stench of death. The corpse spoke with words that were long and drawn out. 'He-e-e knows-s-s!' it said. The words drifted on a whispered breeze. 'He's-s using you. Your soul is in terrible danger-r-r!'

Jack was aghast, not knowing whether he wanted to shoot the monstrosity or run. 'What do you want?' He ventured to ask, unsure of his own eyes. The sound of his voice resonated within his head like an echo.

Everything was still as time became immobile, and the only things in existence were Jack and the boy. He was afraid. What was happening had no substantial bearing on reality.

'Do not fear! This is merely a representation of what I have become. I now exist as both flesh and spirit,' it said. Jack watched, disbelieving, as shadows materialised in the air, grasping at the child's corpse. 'You are being used!' the dead boy said again. 'My father, the Bokor, is responsible, for he now controls all of the dead!'

As Jack was about to question the dead boy, he vanished, leaving Jack alone with the birds singing in the trees. He felt depleted of energy and collapsed on the ground. In his mind, he asked himself whether he was going mad, or perhaps there was a growth in his head that was twisting its malign presence into his consciousness. He had heard of such things before, but the concept was just too weird for him to deal with at the moment. Hell, it was too weird for him to deal with at all! Recovering from his experience, Jack walked back to the cottage.

When Kerry woke, she couldn't find Jack. Her instant reaction was to panic. Assuming he was dead, she waited for them to come back for her. The sound of the latch being raised on the door caused her heart to beat faster and when someone walked in she stifled a scream. Looking again, she saw that it was Jack. Almost crying, she asked, 'Where the hell have you been?'

'What's wrong?' Jack asked, concerned.

'Nothing!' she snapped. 'I thought you... I didn't know what to think. I woke and you were gone. I feared the worst!'

'I went for a walk,' he said, adding, 'I thought I heard a sound and went to investigate. Anyway, I think it's time we started moving.'

The Wailing Banshee was a country pub, and the first sign of civilisation within a twenty-five-mile radius. It was situated on the corner of the road, nestled back amongst trees. It was nearly as secluded as Kerry's cottage. Jack retained a nagging feeling that they were being watched. It was common practice for Sabre Teams from the SAS to patrol the open border.

The pub, though picturesque in location, was typical of the

sectarian watering holes found on the southern side of the border. Though it was early in the evening, the pub had its regular customers dotted around the bar. The air was thick with stale tobacco smoke, and men were seated at tables indulging in games of cards and dominoes. The round, wooden tables were littered with pints of Guinness.

A hostile hush came over the pub as they entered. Here the eyes that were trained upon them identified them as strangers. Those eyes appeared tense and wary.

O'Reilly sat in a darkened corner, observing them coolly. He was a squat man, heavily muscled. His chin was clean-shaven, but his top lip sported a growth of hair that hadn't quite made it into a moustache. He stood up, indicating to Kerry to join him. She looked nervous, and O'Reilly scrutinised her, his face remaining impassive.

Jack was less concerned with O'Reilly; his attention instead fixed upon the two men sitting either side of him; one he could see clearly, but the other's face was concealed by shadows. 'Well, ye've got balls, I'll say that much for ya, Kerry O'Moore! And ta bring ya man with ye, as well!'

Jack stiffened, feeling the cold steel of a gun pushed into the back of his neck. A gentle prod instructed him to move forward. Jack could sense Kerry's dread. Now he had to tread carefully if he was going to maintain any credence. He spoke with a sharp arrogant edge.

'May I sit?'

O'Reilly smiled, mildly amused at Jack's suggestion. Re-taking his seat, he observed Jack with calculating eyes; giving a toothless grin.

'Aye, sit, ya Para bastard. It might be the last time ya will be doin' so!' Jack sat down.

He knew the hatred for the British ran deep and he knew that hatred ran even deeper for the Parachute Regiment. Bloody Sunday had bred that hatred still further. 'I'm no longer in the army,' he stated. At the edge of his vision, Jack glimpsed the shadow-man stir.

'Once a soldier, always a fucking British soldier!' O'Reilly said, expecting a response. Jack maintained eye contact.

'Is it the Parachute Regiment you have the problem with or just me?'

O'Reilly's top lip curled and his eyes became mere pinpricks. The situation had been reversed: the antagonist had become the antagonised.

'All fucking Brit soldiers!' he spat. There was little disguising the contempt in his words. 'What's to stop me from killing ya right here and now?'

Jack realised how precarious his situation had become; the playful banter of words had turned nasty. He sensed Kerry's fear as she stood beside him. Giving a casual glance, he said. 'Too many witnesses?'

O'Reilly gave a hearty laugh, echoed by O'Reilly's companion and the man pushing the gun in the base of Jack's neck.

'You're a comedian and ye've got balls, I'll give ya that much! But ya see, no one here will see a thing!' Jack smiled, intending to call O'Reilly's bluff, drawing him deeper into the yarn he was spinning.

'Well I'm waiting!' Jack placed his hands on the table, palms up. There was raucous laughter from around him.

'I like ye style, Jacob me lad! Ye walk in here bold as brass, with me goddaughter. And I asks meself, what would ye be wanting? Safe haven, is what I'm thinking. Hiding with the enemy. Ya see, we already know all about you, Jacob Portello. Wanted for murder! Ya took a chance coming this far, and, if I was honest with meself, I think it's a bloody miracle!'

Jack instantly decided to press the issue further. 'There!' he said. 'We do have something in common, after all! Both of us hate the British Army. Surely that's the beginnings of an alliance, if not a friendship!'

The Irishman studied Jack with a calculating stare; Jack's eyes never wavered as O'Reilly thought. 'Plus…' Jack reached his hand slowly into his inside pocket. He felt the man behind him tense as the muzzle of the gun was pushed further into his neck. O'Reilly held up his hand as Jack produced a compact disk. 'This!'

O'Reilly looked at the CD as if it were a bomb. 'What's this?' he enquired.

'It's the reason why I'm here. The reason that made me look you up! You see, Kerry here was a means to an end. And that end is here with you!' O'Reilly looked even more perplexed. 'On this disk is information I have acquired from our illustrious intelligence organisation. It contains a detailed description of you, not to mention your many nefarious activities and associations. But what intrigued me most was the stuff I found regarding an organisation called the Fist of Euskadi.' Jack saw the shadow-man shift.

O'Reilly nodded to the man sitting beside him, who produced a small attaché case, which he placed on the table. On opening, it revealed a laptop computer. Placing the disk in the drive, he tapped a few keys before he pushed the case before O'Reilly.

'How did you get this?' O'Reilly's eyes became suspicious once again, alert for the slightest signs of a pitfall.

'If you've checked me out, then you will know that I'm a hacker. It's a skill I acquired in the army. I came by this information by sheer accident. Hopefully a lucrative accident? I was trying to erase myself from military and governmental databases when I came across this. I assumed the information would be of worth to someone, so I downloaded it.'

'So you run to me! Why? Is it money, or do you want to escape the country? Or is it work ye be looking for? Haven't you heard the cause is dead? It's all over, save the signing on the dotted line!'

Jack smiled. 'I'm not interested in joining the cause – a dead cause, as you put it! That disk also holds detailed accounts on an organisation known as the Fist of Euskadi. It's them I'm really interested in.' Jack heard the pub door open and close behind him.

A man dressed in a black duffel coat and a woolly hat joined them. Jack recognised Duffy, the man he had met at Bradbury Lines. No eye contact passed between them, and Duffy remained aloof.

The shadow-man leant forward, his face in plain view for the first time. Jack instantly recognised him as Felix Grouper. His face looked like it had been chiselled out of granite; cruel lines carved his features. His hair was blond, closely cropped and shaven at the back and sides. Jack saw a genetic by-product of an insane Germany: fragments of ludicrous ideals perversely blown out of proportion, creating an Aryan Frankenstein.

The shadow-man whispered in O'Reilly's ear. 'It seems that ye've impressed me friend here! But I've learnt to be cautious in me old age; it's how I've survived for as long as I have. So how do I know that this is not some kind of SAS sting?'

Jack went cold. He had to think fast, deciding to call the other man's bluff. 'You don't!' he said with a smile. Grouper bellowed with laughter.

'I like your style, Englishman! I can see now why your people won both World Wars!' His accent was heavy.

Turning his attention to Grouper, Jack eyed him suspiciously. 'I don't believe we've been introduced.'

'You're bold, you're straightforward, and you come here demanding to be heard. Somehow I think there is more to you than meets the eye!' Grouper said, with a questioning look on his face.

'You might be right!' Jack made to rise from his seat when he felt firm hands grip his shoulders. Taking the hint, he relaxed in his seat once more.

'What's your hurry?' Grouper asked, beginning to chuckle. Jack studied his eyes. They were those of a man gone too far.

'It's obvious I'm wasting my time here,' Jack said.

Grouper held up his large paw. 'Not so fast, my friend. You came here seeking Euskadi. What price would you pay? How high would you go? Would you sell your soul to enter the land of devils?'

Jack's eyes narrowed as he evaluated the man before him. Smiling, he said, 'If the price were right! I sold my soul a long time ago and perhaps it's time I reneged on that deal!' Grouper began to laugh again.

'The price will be right, I assure you!' Jack half smiled, trying to share Grouper's personal joke.

'It may be stupidity on my part, but I didn't get who you were.'

Grouper leaned forward, resting his large forearms on the table. He brought his face within inches of Jack's. Jack could smell peppermint on his breath. 'I am the guardian of the Underworld, The gatekeeper, if you will, and I will be your guide in the dungeons of hell!' Jack leaned back in his seat.

'This may all make a very good bedtime story, but I came here prepared to sell information. I had hoped that Mr O'Reilly could help me, but it seems that I was mistaken.'

'Don't be too hasty,' Grouper smiled. 'Who I am is not of importance at this time. It may be fortuitous for you to have come when you did. Men of good military standing seldom come onto the market, and men with the ability to lead even less. Tell me, you used to be in the Parachute Regiment – which division?'

'The Pathfinder Platoon,' Jack replied, seeing recognition light in the man's eye.

'Prestigious!' Grouper said. 'Let me tell you a little bit about the organisation you call the Fist of Euskadi. It is a group of freedom fighters who want to free their country from tyranny.'

'The Basque country,' Jack interrupted. 'Have you ever heard of a man named Égalité?' Grouper's face became stern. 'Only there was a lot of information about him in connection to the Fist of Euskadi?'

Grouper grabbed the laptop, scanning the content. 'His is not the only name contained on this disk. You are an interesting fellow, Jacob Portello…'

'Jack. Call me Jack.'

'Jack. Captain, Pathfinder Platoon, working with the 16 Air Assault Brigade's advance force. Operations to insert combat units before any air assault operation, providing covert reconnaissance, location drop zones and helicopter landing sites. Trained for both air and vehicle insertion. Arrested for treason in 2000 and sentenced to life. Known to the Real IRA as 'Trooper'. You trade in information, do you not? Selling to the highest bidder. You escaped from military prison one week ago, killing three guards in your escape. Need I go on?' Jack remained silent but apprehensive. 'It seems, Jack, that we have more in common than we originally thought. We are the same – men used to a strict military routine and with murder not too far from our minds.' Grouper nodded. 'Mr O'Reilly here and his associates seem very interested in something we have to offer. You, in turn, have something to offer me. Things may just turn out to be of benefit to all concerned.' He addressed everybody at the table.

O'Reilly smiled. 'Be here tomorrow at seven sharp, Jack!'

Jack noticed Grouper eyeing Kerry. He reminded Jack of a spider with a fly entangled in its web. 'And bring the delightful Miss O'Moore with you as well. She brightens this dreary place like a fiery flower!' Grouper added.

Jack rose from his seat. As he did so, he spotted Duffy standing at the bar. 'Until tomorrow then!' O'Reilly said to his back. Jack and Kerry walked calmly out the pub.

O'Reilly turned to Felix Grouper, his face a mask of incredulity. 'Surely you don't believe him do you?'

Grouper looked at O'Reilly. 'Is there any reason why I should doubt his sincerity – he is a man in need, willing to trade information. We can aid his need, and in return he will aid ours.' O'Reilly went red in the face, his anger becoming visible; he vented it in a furious outburst.

'But he's a fucking Brit! A Para! I could never work with an organisation that worked with the enemy!'

'Mr Égalité encourages tolerance of other ethnic cultures and religions, as should you.' O'Reilly's top lip curled as he snarled.

'And what if I don't want to?'

No one saw Felix Grouper's hand move – he was fast – and O'Reilly stared down the barrel of an Ingram submachine pistol.

O'Reilly began to laugh. 'Do ye really believe that ye will be walking out of here?'

Grouper smiled back. 'Well, one thing's for certain: you will not! And if anything happens to me, it's not the British Army you need worry about: it will be Mr Égalité. Because you and the whole of your piss pot IRA will be spread so far apart that the British Army will be finding pieces of it for the next fifty years!'

O'Reilly's face went white; he had done his homework before deciding to make a bid for the weapon. The Fist of Euskadi, though virtually unheard of outside militant circles, had a reputation. The group comprised of highly-trained military personnel, dissenters worldwide who dealt in an efficient and deadly manner with people who crossed them.

O'Reilly held up his hands in mock surrender. 'Hey, I was only kidding!'

Grouper lay the submachine gun on the table and smiled a toothy grin. 'So was I!' he said. 'But if you're that worried that Mr Portello and Miss O'Moore are not genuine, then I have an idea that will draw them out one way or the other.' Grouper smiled, knowingly. 'Send in the hounds and see which way they run!'

Chapter 7

During the journey back to Kerry's hide-away cottage, Jack's mind was troubled. O'Reilly's casual but explicit mention of the SAS worried him. He knew the Irish were a mistrustful bunch and that they feared the SAS above all other British military establishments.

The cottage appeared unchanged as they walked along the grove to the secluded building. Jack was cautious, viewing the property with suspicion, sensing something was not right. Placing a cautionary hand on Kerry's shoulder, he placed himself before her. 'There's someone here!' he whispered. Kerry looked at him, fear written in her eyes.

Drawing the Browning, Jack stood back, slamming his foot into the door. The lock gave way, splintering from its mounting as the door swung open. Gun raised in a two-handed grip, Jack's finger was poised on the trigger guard, taking up the fraction of slack on the trigger itself.

Nonchalantly, Herbert Duff walked down the stairs as Jack lowered his gun. 'You could have been shot!'

Duffy flashed a smile. 'Well, what kind of a greeting is that?'

'A deadly one!' Jack said, inciting another smile from Duffy as he placed a half-smoked cigarette between his lips.

'I've been instructed to keep an eye on you! I also thought I'd better tell you to expect a visit, later tonight!'

'A visit?' Kerry queried, her anxiety growing. 'What do you mean, a visit?'

Duffy's attention remained on Jack. 'Let's just say that a test has been arranged by mutual acquaintances!'

Understanding immediately dawned on Jack. 'You mean that the lions have been loosed, to see which way we run?'

Duffy gave Jack a wink and a knowing smile. 'I'll see myself out now that I know you've got home safely!'

Placing a woolly hat on his head, he began to whistle 'Rule,

Britannia!' and walked out of the cottage. As Jack watched him go, Kerry moved alongside him, the question in her mind suddenly bursting from her lips. 'What did he mean?'

Jack explained that Duffy was undercover. 'He's just told me that your godfather has arranged a little visit to see if we are kosher or not!' An uneasy silence descended between the two of them.

Time passed slowly, and Kerry observed Jack sitting in her father's old rocking chair. He looked to be asleep; his eyes were closed as he rocked gently back and forth, a gun nestled in his lap. 'I think we should get out of here,' she suggested, when Jack opened his eyes a fraction.

'If we did that, the game's up. O'Reilly would know that this was a sting operation, and we would never get anywhere near him or the Fist of Euskadi again. Besides, I am curious to know exactly what he has planned. It will give me a feel for the man, an insight as to how his mind works.'

Kerry was aghast. Rising from her seat, she approached a wooden desk. Opening one of the drawers, she slipped her hand inside. A hollow click followed, as a concealed compartment opened to reveal a gun. The weapon was a Smith & Wesson .38 Special.

It appeared to be well oiled, and Kerry unclasped the breech, breaking the handgun open. Checking it was loaded, she spun the chamber before locking the breech back in place. Jack watched, mildly interested, closing his eyes again when she had finished.

As daylight dwindled, Kerry looked at Jack. 'I can't take much more of this,' she said, after a while.

'You'll wish we were still waiting when it arrives!' Jack stated, dryly.

Perceiving movement beyond the window, Jack listened intently, hearing the muffled snap of a twig being crushed underfoot. Kerry, oblivious to what was happening, felt Jack pull her to her feet. Maintaining a hold of her gun, she allowed herself to be propelled through the house.

The cold air stung her cheeks, the danger exhilarating, but riding above all this was raw fear. Jack stopped. A void of darkness smothered them as Kerry was left alone, contemplating a scarcely definable silhouette dwindling into the gloom.

Embracing her gun, Kerry gingerly scanned the darkness. She felt detached and powerless, the gun offering little reassurance as she could barely see a thing. The gloom closed in around her as she expectantly waited for Jack to return.

There was a muffled noise behind her, and she felt a thick forearm encircle her neck. A menacing voice whispered in her ear. 'Where's the Brit?' The sharp point of a knife dug into her neck. Fear washed through her as she stammered, 'I… I… don't know!'

The thick silence abruptly shattered with the sound of sirens. Racing along the grove towards the cottage was a trail of headlights with flashing blue beacons. Kerry noted a moment's hesitation in her captor, and she jabbed her elbow back, hard. There was a grunt, and the hold released. Free, Kerry raced blindly into the darkness.

As Kerry ran, she was confronted by jerking flashlights. Coming to a standstill, a hand muffled her mouth, pulling her back into the tree line. 'It's me!' Jack whispered in her ear. 'We've got to get out of here!' Taking her hand, he guided her through the blackened maze of trees.

Breaking free of the woods, headlights dazzled their vision as Jack immediately dived to the ground, pulling Kerry with him. The vehicle slowed to a halt alongside their position, and Jack looked up to see O'Reilly's face, grinning at him. 'You bastard! You set this up!' Jack said.

'It was a test, Jack, me lad! Just to see whose side you're really on! No hard feelings, I hope?' He grinned, as Jack clambered off the floor, pulling Kerry to her feet. Duffy sat behind the steering wheel, his face a mask of hostility. Jack and Kerry jumped into the back of the stationary vehicle before it raced away.

'Where are we going?' Jack asked, receiving no reply.

Sharply pulling off the road, Duffy navigated them into a nearby field, where a helicopter waited with its rotors spinning.

The whistle of the engines screeched into the night as Jack settled himself into his seat, and the helicopter lifted into the star-filled sky.

They flew into Dublin airport, where a Boeing 767 awaited their arrival. Grouper stood at the foot of the boarding stairs. 'Welcome!'

he said, smiling and nodding in Jack's direction. 'Now is the proper time for me to introduce myself! My name is Felix Grouper, and I apologise for any inconvenience caused!' Grouper indicated the aircraft with his hand. 'If you would all like to follow me!'

They followed Grouper up the stairs into the body of the craft. O'Reilly looked uncomfortable, and there was a questioning expression on his face. Grouper stood in the aisle. 'Please take a seat and fasten your seat belts. We will be departing shortly!' He made his way towards the front of the plane.

Sitting down, O'Reilly said, 'I don't know what's going on; this was not the arrangement!' He looked at Jack like he had the answers, when Grouper appeared before them.

'There is no need to concern yourself, Mr O'Reilly; things have just been brought forward a little. The auction is taking place in a few days, and you will all be my honoured guests.'

O'Reilly glared, his eyes demanding answers. 'And where exactly would you be taking us?'

'Don't worry, Mr O'Reilly! Let me reassure you that everything will be in order when we touch down. Just think of it as a holiday for which we will be picking up the tab.'

'You'll reassure me of nothing. I haven't stayed alive for as long as I have without worrying and covering me own arse!'

The vibration of the jet engines was felt by all aboard, and gradually the craft began to move, progressively increasing its speed. Jack felt his stomach lunge as the plane took off. When the craft was safely in the air, Grouper enquired if anyone would like a drink. As he disappeared, Jack looked towards O'Reilly. 'What's going on?' he asked, his voice restrained.

'Your guess is as good as mine!' O'Reilly replied, shrugging his broad shoulders.

'You trust him?'

O'Reilly gave a toothless smirk that aged his reddened and chubby face.

'I trust him about as much as I trust you, Jack me lad!'

Jack couldn't help but give a coarse smile as Grouper returned, carrying a tray of drinks.

'Where are we going?' Jack asked. Grouper mindfully watched him.

'You will see when we arrive!'

'Are we being kidnapped?'

Grouper chuckled. 'As I said, you are our honoured guests.' Grouper made himself comfortable sipping his drink. 'I believe I am going to enjoy working with you, Jack. You have a very dry sense of humour, not unlike my own.'

Jack smiled. 'Why, are you offering me employment?'

Grouper laughed, his gaze falling on Duffy, who did not appear pleased. 'Why the glum face, Irish?' Duffy's eyes lingered on the South African, but he remained aloof.

Things had gone wrong. The original strategy to insert Jack into the Fist of Euskadi was still going to plan, but the involvement of Duffy and Kerry had not been considered.

Jack knew that Duffy would be adept at improvisation, but he had his doubts regarding Kerry. She was seated, silent and subdued, trying to disappear into the seat she sat in. Jack was all too aware of the fear she felt. She was being propelled forward into an uncertain future that held no familiarity for her.

Kerry reached out her hand, taking hold of Jack's. In a way, he was glad to be able to comfort her. In fact, Jack detected an air of despondency within the craft. He couldn't help noticing the worried and haggard complexion of O'Reilly; only a few hours ago, he had been the staunch Provisional Republican with an air of self-righteousness about him. Now his eyes had become jittery.

Breaking the uncomfortable silence, Grouper stood up. 'I would like to propose a toast!' he said. 'To new friends!' The response was lacklustre, but everybody raised their glasses.

Relaxing, Jack drifted on clouds of his own subconscious. He opened his eyes to find Grouper violently shaking him. When he saw that Jack was awake, he smiled, revealing white and uneven teeth. 'I thought you were dead then, Jack. You were so cold.'

'What time is it?' Jack asked.

'It's time to wake up; we're coming in to land.'

Jack felt strange; an electric current was rushing the length of his spine, and a pulsation in his head pounded like beating drums. He felt faint, the surrounding air constraining him. Regulating his breathing, he willed the sensations and sounds away. As the aircraft taxied to a standstill, Jack briefly glanced out of the portside window, knowing exactly where he was.

The flight had lasted just over six hours, and they had landed at Diori Hamani airport in Niamey, the capital city of Niger. There was no need to check into Customs, as two limousines waited for their arrival on the runway. As Jack clambered into the first, he thought that whatever had happened in the past was where it must remain. This was the here and now, and he had to concentrate on the job in hand.

Jack accompanied Grouper and O'Reilly in the first limousine. Duffy and Kerry would be following in the second. O'Reilly sat next to Grouper, while Jack faced them both. 'It's like a new adventure!' Grouper said with a smile.

As the vehicles meandered their way through the streets of Niamey, Jack realised how little the city had changed; the metropolis had an air of ruin about it.

The limousines drew to a halt before a grand hotel. A large sign proclaimed 'Le Souverain Natal'. Jack smiled at the irony. Native Sovereign, he thought. A porter approached the car, opening the door. He touched the peak of his cap on seeing Grouper.

Jack took particular notice of people's reactions when around Grouper; he observed that their salutations were not given freely – fear resided in their eyes. Jack also saw the satisfaction it gave Grouper, as if he were feeding from their fear.

Grouper lead them to the elevators located in the lobby. 'Your apartments have been made ready,' Grouper stated, as the elevator car stopped on the tenth floor.

As the doors, opened Jack couldn't believe his eyes. Hovering above him was the face of the tribal witch doctor as he had seen him after the attack. That same face stood before him now, staring straight into his eyes. Jack's training took command as he walked out of the elevator. 'Don't mind Samdi,' Grouper grinned. 'He's just something I picked up on a hunting expedition!' Grouper rapped his knuckles on Samdi's forehead. Jack saw a bitterness in the other man's eyes. 'He thinks he's some kind of mighty voodoo witch doctor, but his shit don't work on non-believers!'

'*Houngan*!' Jack said suddenly, his mind seeing the figure silhouetted by the sun after the attack in Cameroon. Was Grouper the man responsible for the carnage that occurred there? Surely that would be too much of a coincidence.

'What?' he asked, as Jack grappled with himself, bringing his mind back into the present.

'A voodoo priest is a *Houngan*!' Jack said. Grouper waved his hand; Jack's comment meant nothing.

'Kaffir, show these people to their rooms!' Grouper stepped back into the elevator, leaving them alone.

'There are rooms for all,' Samdi said, his eyes never withdrawing from Jack. 'Follow me!'

Samdi led them down a corridor with a plush red carpet, pausing outside the first of the rooms. 'This is to be your room, miss.' He opened the door wide, allowing Kerry a view of the interior.

A white wool carpet stretched out across the expanse of the room. There was a high-class leather-upholstered settee and chairs. A large plasma screen was mounted on the wall, and there was a minibar with drinks provided. Samdi, looking at Kerry, said, 'I hope it meets with your approval?' Kerry nodded, stepping into the room and closing the door behind her.

'Which is my room?' O'Reilly asked.

'The next apartment is yours.'

O'Reilly held out his hand for the key and Samdi obliged.

'Be Jesus!' was all they heard from O'Reilly as they passed by his room. The next room had been allocated to Duffy, who entered without saying a word. Jack proceeded to follow Samdi to the next apartment, permitting him to open the door.

'And this is your room, Mr Portello; or should I say Mr Jack Hornsby?'

Jack was interrupted mid-stride as he set foot in the room, the disturbance manifesting on his face, and he slowly turned round.

'In fact, I was wondering when you would get here!' Samdi spoke with a clipped upper-class British accent, and Jack frowned at the man before him. Samdi's face was long, with hollow cheekbones. It was a countenance that was barren of emotion. He began to walk away, but Jack grabbed his shoulder, roughly turning him round.

'What did you say?' Jack's face was askew with distrust, but

Samdi refused to answer, shrugging free of Jack's grasp with ease.

Walking away, he said, 'All in good time, Jack!' and chuckled. 'All in good time!'

Transfixed by shock, Jack watched Samdi calmly walk back along the corridor, astonished at the ease with which he had shrugged free of his grasp. It would be pointless instigating further confrontation. It was apparent the man knew exactly who he was. How was a mystery; how many others knew besides him?

Jack walked into his apartment, questions forming in his mind. Walking directly to the minibar, he located a bottle of five-star brandy and drank it neat, directly from the bottle. Sitting down, a remote control lay on the armrest; he turned the set on. CNN news flashed onto the screen. It depicted yet another terrorist attack, this time in Germany. Jack hit the off switch, feeling unsettled.

Events ran through Jack's mind and he found himself slipping into tranquillity. His eyes became heavy. His repose was invaded by Samdi pointing a finger and Grouper realising he had been duped. Jack dreamt of his own death as a cloud of radiation spread its lethal touch across the globe.

Repetitive knocking at the door roused him. Sunbeams shone through the window in hot golden streams, warming his face. Climbing off the bed, the empty bottle of brandy tumbled to the floor.

He raked his fingers through his hair, disengaging the door. Grouper stood in the doorway, a cordial smile on his face. 'Good evening!' he said, offering Jack a tray laden with steaming coffee and toast.

'What time is it?' Jack asked.

'6 p.m. Mr Égalité has expressed a desire to meet with you. He will be waiting in the cocktail lounge.' Jack nodded an acknowledgement, and, without further discussion, Grouper left.

After a shower and a shave, Jack felt rejuvenated; he dressed in clothes that he found in his room.

Directions to the lounge were posted, along with arrows showing the way. Jack passed a restaurant. Stairs swept down on either side to the dining area on a level below. Following the signs, Jack located the lounge. The doors were open, and he entered, discovering a circular room. It was like a mini stadium, with spiral steps that led down to a bar, seats, tables and a cabaret area. Jack saw Grouper, his elbow propped on the bar. He was not alone: a thin man in a white suit and fedora hat sat at one of the tables, with a long drink before him. The brim of his hat cast his eyes in shadow.

As Jack observed him sipping his drink, the man stood up, acknowledging his presence. Slowly Jack descended, gaining a clearer view of the man. His eyes were the most prominent feature of his face; hypnotic in their stare, they undulated within the artificial light. Jack recognised Phillip Égalité from the photograph he had seen back in Hereford. He was not as grand as his title of King Terrorist suggested. His face was gaunt and hollow, as if the man were malnourished, but Jack saw in his eyes that he considered himself to be superior in every way.

He removed his hat before re-seating himself, uncovering a shock of black, Mediterranean hair that was frosted with grey. Jack smiled as warmly as he could. From the corner of his vision, he saw that someone else stood in the lounge with them; his head was bowed in silent prayer as he stood amongst the shadows. Égalité spoke.

'You must be Captain Jacob Portello. Let me introduce myself; I am Phillip Égalité.'

As Jack confronted him, Égalité looked him in the eye. 'I believe that you have information that you wish to share with me.'

Staring back, Jack laughed. 'There's no profit in sharing!'

Égalité smiled, passing a transient glance at Grouper. 'The root of all evil. If only money had never been invented!' His face grew sad. 'So, Jack… You don't mind if I call you Jack, do you? What is your price?'

Jack remained thoughtful. 'That depends on what the information is worth to you. Shall we start at a nice round figure of say – I don't know – ten million sterling?'

'You wish me to bid? And may I ask whom I am bidding against?'

Jack smiled. 'The Fist of Euskadi. I'm sure they would be most interested, since most of the information contained on that disk is about them.'

Égalité was mildly amused. 'My dear Jack…' Égalité and

Grouper began to laugh. Jack looked at them both. 'I apologise for laughing, but you see, Felix and I, that is, we *are* the Fist of Euskadi. We created the movement as a front to divert attention away from our business transactions. So, unless you expect Felix to bid against me, then there is no other potential buyer. Now, I have a suggestion: we will pay you five million now, and an additional ten million if you complete a little task for me.'

Jack frowned. 'Task?'

'There are certain files held by the British Government that are of great interest to me…' Jack had no idea where Égalité was going. 'Information regarding the movement of certain dignitaries. To a man such as yourself, this should be no great task. I will have a list given to you later.'

Their conversation was halted as Kerry walked into the lounge. As she approached, Jack was immersed with guilt: he was responsible for involving her. Since that night with Kerry, his emotions were divided. He felt that he needed to shield her. She had almost reached them when Égalité rose from his seat.

'A pleasure, my dear!' Kerry smiled politely as Égalité took her hand and kissed it. A look of repulsion manifested on her face as she retreated to Jack's side. Égalité smiled cordially. 'Such a delicate flower! I do hope that you have not been too inconvenienced, Miss O'Moore, but expediency was vitally important, or so Felix informed me!'

Raised voices came from above, and there were sounds of a scuffle at the entrance to the lounge. Duffy was thrust through the doors, followed by two brawny men with shaven heads. They roughly manhandled him down the walkway and stood like a pair of well-trained Rottweilers before Égalité.

'Call off your guard dogs!' Duffy stated bluntly, trying to shake loose the two men. Grouper watched, an ugly grin poised on his lips. He raised his hand, and Duffy was thrown to the floor.

'What's going on here?' Duffy demanded, facing Felix Grouper. Grouper remained impassive, more amused than angered by this scrawny Irishman as Égalité spoke in a soothing voice.

'I don't believe we have been introduced. My name is Phillip Égalité, and you are?'

'Patrick McDuff! I was following her down…' – he nodded

towards Kerry – '…until these two bruisers got hold of me!' Duffy's accusing eyes rested on his two attackers.

'I must apologise for the over-impulsive actions of my staff, but they do have a job to do, and that is to protect me! You can go now!' The two men took their leave. 'Oh, and if you could do one small thing for me…' he called after them. 'Could you collect Mr O'Reilly from his room and bring him to me? Thank you!'

Looking back at Duffy, he said, 'Now where were we? You are Mr O'Reilly's personal aide?'

'Something like that,' Duffy replied.

'Good!' Égalité said, clapping his hands together. 'When Mr O'Reilly arrives we can begin.'

When Shamus O'Reilly staggered through the door, he had to be supported. The man looked a mess: his clothes hung unfastened about his person, and his eyes were bloodshot from too much drink.

'We found him like this, sir!' one of the men explained. Égalité nodded in both an acknowledgement and a dismissal. Grouper observed all from his position by the bar, amusement written all over his face.

O'Reilly fell back onto one of the chairs. Minuscule red veins blemished his cheeks and nose as he looked out through bleary eyes. Grouper stifled a chuckle at the bar.

'You must be me man, Égalité. I have been waiting a long time to meet ye!' O'Reilly's slurred speech, combined with his thick Irish brogue, was difficult to follow.

'It seems Mr O'Reilly has discovered the delights of our apartment bars,' Égalité remarked, turning his attention to Duffy. 'I've brought you here to explain that the auction will begin in seventy-two hours. Other interested parties will be arriving as the day continues. The delights of this hotel are at your disposal. Feel free to explore. If you'll excuse me, I have pressing issues to attend to!'

Égalité departed the lounge along with Grouper. O'Reilly had fallen asleep on the chair and was snoring softly.

'Jack?' Kerry muttered. 'What is going on here? And what have I been dragged into?'

'You've got to go back!' Jack voiced categorically. 'I'll see if I can't persuade Égalité to put you on a plane home.'

Chapter 8

Duffy caught up with Jack in the lobby of the hotel, just as the elevator doors slid open. They stepped inside. Duffy was about to speak when Jack surreptitiously nudged him. He had spotted an innocuous-looking sphere in the corner. Duffy traced his line of sight and immediately understood.

When they stepped out and the doors had begun to close, Duffy spoke in a low and hushed voice. 'You think the place is bugged?' Jack smiled and kept his eyes dead ahead, making an agreeing sound.

As Duffy entered his apartment, he heard Jack's door close. They had both reached the same conclusion: the hotel was bugged. It was not inconceivable that they were being watched as well as listened to. They had arranged to meet at nightfall out on the balcony. The background noise of the city would add confusion to any overheard discussions.

Just as Duffy settled, there was an urgent knocking at his door. O'Reilly stood on the other side, recovered from his hangover. 'Where've you been?' he asked.

'In my room,' Duffy replied, as O'Reilly pushed him back and closed the door. His face was stern, and he held his finger to his lips. Guiding Duffy by the arm, he directed him to the French doors that led out onto the balcony.

Outside, a warm breeze caressed their faces, and O'Reilly spoke in undertones. 'Something's bothering me! It don't feel right here, like I'm being watched.' Duffy smiled, preparing a speech in his head that would quell O'Reilly's fears.

'What will ye expect?' Duffy said, turning on his Irish intonation. 'Men like Mr Égalité and Mr Grouper would want security to be of the highest quality. If we had the funds available to us, we'd do the same.'

O'Reilly nodded his head. 'I suppose you're right, but I don't like changes and being dragged away from me beloved Emerald

Isle. I'm having meself some doubts, Patrick me lad. Can't help feeling that I've made a mistake!' He shook his head. 'I've believed in the cause since I was knee-high. I've not always agreed with what has been done in its name, but after a while it becomes more than that. It eats away at your soul, Patrick, to the point that winning becomes everything, no matter the cost!' O'Reilly held his head in his hands. 'Oh God, forgive me for what I have started!' the Irishman said to himself, walking out of the apartment.

Light had deserted the sky, and Duffy stood looking out of the open French doors, a fresh wind blowing in his face, as Jack stepped out of the shadows. 'Seems your man O'Reilly's getting unsettled!'

'You heard then,' Duffy said, walking onto the balcony and gazing down at the city below. 'O'Reilly's not the only one! I'm not supposed to be here, remember?'

'Things go wrong. You know that as well as I do!'

Duffy turned to Jack. 'This isn't like a normal operation!'

'We've still been trained for it.'

'I don't mean it that way. Something feels odd about it… Like strings are being pulled somewhere.'

'My room's definitely bugged,' Jack said.

Duffy nodded. 'Mine too. You know this is a right fuck up! This is Ferguson's turf, not mine!'

A thought began to form in Jack's mind. 'We might be able to use this to our advantage. I sense that Grouper doesn't trust you, and this should afford you a freedom that I won't have.'

'You mean I become the middleman?' Duffy asked.

Jack flashed a smile. 'Exactly! There's a French café in the city called *Le Garer*; it's near to the British Embassy. Be there in two days at 17.00 hours. The café's on…' There came a resounding knock from Jack's apartment which was shortly followed by a knock at Duffy's door.

'I'll find it!' Duffy confirmed, moving back into his room and slipping his trousers down around his ankles and pulling them up again. With one hand, he answered the door.

A tall man, over six feet, wearing a long, dour face, confronted Duffy as he smiled, faking embarrassment. 'I'm having a slight problem with these here trousers!' he said, watching as the man dropped his gaze slightly to Duffy's hand.

Jack climbed back onto his balcony when he heard the door to his apartment open. Leaning on the balcony, he looked out across Niamey. He was conscious that someone was approaching from behind. Instinctively, his muscles bunched, as a voice said, 'Is there a problem, Jack?'

'No,' he replied, in a surprised manner. 'Should there be?'

Grouper viewed him quizzically. 'I knocked and you didn't answer.'

Jack smiled. 'I was just gazing, remembering the way things used to be!'

Grouper chuckled. 'Too many regrets?'

'Too many things not to regret!' Jack laughed.

Grouper slapped him on the back. 'Dinner is being served!'

Jack followed Grouper, spotting Duffy lingering by the elevators. A curt nod passed between him and Grouper.

Entering the restaurant, Jack saw Égalité sitting at the top table; from his position he could oversee the entire restaurant. Jack scanned the rest of the room. It was almost full, and the diversity of the people there was astounding. Jack spotted Chinese Triads, South Americans, possibly Cubans and people from the Middle East, all accompanied by their own personal entourage of bodyguards. Grouper led Jack directly to Égalité's table where Kerry and O'Reilly were seated, perusing a menu. When Égalité saw them, he rose from his seat with a broad smile. Jack felt apprehensive.

'We thought you had got lost!' Égalité laughed, as they approached the table. Grouper sat by Égalité, imparting a few words in his ear. This appeared to amuse Égalité. A broad grin spread across his face.

'I can recommend all of the dishes to be found on this menu – they are all first class!'

Grouper indicated for a waiter to approach, as Égalité sat with a smug expression on his face. 'Our hotel is the most prestigious and exclusive building in Niger! I like to surround myself with finery and quality!' His eyes flicked to Grouper momentarily until they settled again on Jack. 'Which is why we are offering you, Jack, a position with us!'

Jack remained silent, his gaze narrowing. 'I haven't decided on that one yet, but I could be persuaded if the price were right.'

Égalité waved his hand in a dismissive manner.

'I'm not talking about figures, Jacob. The amount should far exceed your meagre salary from the British Army. No! What I am talking about is commitment and duty. Honour is so hard to find in the modern world. What I am offering is…' Égalité removed a pen from his inside pocket, wrote something on a napkin, and slid it in front of Jack.

The amount far exceeded anything he could have hoped to earn in his entire military service. Jack had to admit he was tempted, but the innocents that had died, and those who would die because of this monster, pulled him into check.

'That is quite an impressive sum, but are you acquiring my fighting skills or my soul?' Grouper began to chuckle, and Jack remembered the conversation he'd had with him back at the Wailing Banshee. Quickly coming back into focus, Jack found himself searching for Samdi.

He spotted him, concealed by shadows, and was sure that his hooded gaze fell directly upon him. He suddenly felt cold and turned his attention to Égalité once more.

'Are you all right?' Égalité asked.

Jack nodded, laughing it off.

'A bit of jet lag.' Reaching forward, he grasped a pitcher of water, poured himself a glass and took a hefty swig.

'Then it is to your approval?' Égalité asked. Jack nodded, faking a smile.

After the meal was finished, they retired to the cocktail lounge, where Égalité revelled in being the host, recounting various humorous stories he had picked up on his extensive travels. There was no direct mention of the Fist of Euskadi throughout the remainder of the evening, until Égalité took Jack to one side.

'Tomorrow, my friend, you will have great delight in viewing the organisation from the inside.'

The evening at a close, Kerry and Jack accompanied both Égalité and Grouper to the elevators. Inserting a key into the control panel, Grouper turned it, and the elevator began to smoothly rise. Jack noted that the number panel indicating floors was not lit, when the elevator came to a sedate standstill, and the doors slid open.

Noting that Grouper removed the key, Jack assumed they had travelled to Égalité's private suite. 'See you soon, Jacob, Miss O'Moore!' Égalité stepped out as the doors began to close. The lift rose another floor before the panel light came on.

Kerry appeared to be unsettled. 'Are you all right?' Jack asked and she gazed into his eyes.

'I am now!' she said. 'Now that I'm with you!' Jack pulled her closer to him as they reached their destination. Stepping out of the elevator, Jack spoke in Kerry's ear.

'It's not safe for you here! I'll try to arrange somewhere safe for you to go.'

They reached the door of Kerry's apartment. Opening it, Kerry tried to lead Jack with her. She sensed a moment's hesitation and stopped, turning around.

'What's wrong?' she asked, touching his cheek lightly with her hand. 'I'm afraid. Won't you stay with me just a while?'

Jack wanted to tell her of his conflicting emotions, about his love for Lisa and his desire for her, but he was aware of the monitoring devices that were in place. Divulging his emotions now could conceivably blow his cover.

Jack slept, yet his subconscious was alert. Sensing movement, his instinct overcame all sluggishness. Jumping out of bed, all was in darkness, but his eyesight rapidly adjusted. The sound had come from the balcony. Jack noiselessly approached the French doors, snatching them open. Duffy confronted him with a sheepish grin balanced on his face. 'I hope I didn't disturb you?'

'What's up?' Jack asked, knowing that this wasn't merely a social call.

'I've just finished talking with O'Reilly, who's had a quaint *tête-à-tête* with Grouper. Grouper's paranoia might be becoming infectious. It appears your instinct was right and the big ape does not like me. O'Reilly's just informed me that, whatever happens, I'm not invited to your little party tomorrow.'

'Did O'Reilly say how many would be going?' Jack asked.

Duffy shook his head. 'I think it's all the bidders, and of course you.'

Jack began to think things through in his mind. It might be better if Duffy tried to locate Ferguson while Jack was away and apprise him of the situation. 'OK. We'll postpone our meeting by two days, but we'll stick to our original time.'

Jack moved back into Kerry's apartment as Duffy slipped away into the darkness.

Chapter 9

Jack's sleep was invaded by abstruse images. The nightmare descended with such brutal deliberation that he grappled to escape its embrace. He looked down upon his own rotting corpse.

Feeling dread on a spiritual level, he heard a chorus rising up and out of the distance. The sound was all-encompassing, undulating with sinister undertones. The words were foreign to his ears, cajoling and taunting in an ancient tongue that left a condemnation upon the spirit. Jack could scarcely see as fog swirled around him, but moving in the mist were shadows: figures dancing. Their faces became distinct within the haze. They were familiar to him. He recognised Égalité, O'Reilly and Kerry, their joyous faces twisted and perverse. Grouper arose out of the swirling mist at Jack's feet. He saw a distorted leer engraved on his lips as he spoke with a venom-infected tongue. 'What's it like to be dead, Jack?' The words receded, as a guttural laughter echoed around him.

Kerry stepped forward, speaking with soft, warm breath that caressed his cold cheek. 'We could have been good together, lover!' She kissed him lightly on the cheek. Then her face was replaced with O'Reilly's countenance.

The Irishman's bloated, blotched cheeks gave him a more ominous semblance. He screamed at Jack, his voice harsh and cruel. 'SAS bastard!' Jack could still hear his wild ranting as he ebbed away into the distance.

Then the smiling visage of Phillip Égalité floated before him, his skin transparent, revealing a serpentine countenance. Emotionless, inimical eyes drew him into a vacuum of melancholy. Égalité spoke with a torrid and underlying loathing. 'Traitor!' he spat. Jack heard laughing. Now Samdi stood before him, dressed in the apparel of a tribal witch doctor. 'Vengeance will be mine!' he stated, laughing in a fevered frenzy.

Jack woke suddenly, his eyes snapping open, struggling against the restraints of his sheets. Slowly the nightmare images subsided.

A knock on the door brought him into focus. A sliver of light crept its way through the curtain; the knock came again. Jack rose from the mattress, climbing into a pair of jeans. 'Room service!' a soft voice called from outside the door.

He was greeted by a young African girl of about eighteen years of age. 'Coffee, sir!' she said with a smile. Jack gratefully accepted, thanking her, and closed the door.

Turning around, he saw Kerry lying in bed, the bed linen softly draped about her body. She stirred, the sheet riding down slightly, revealing her breasts. Jack observed her as he poured himself some coffee. This woman was a complete mystery to him, as if within the glory of her beauty, she held something dark and sinister.

Opening her eyes, their sparkle caught in the morning light. 'Hello, lover!' she said with a smile. Wriggling in bed, she stretched her body to the maximum. Jack went cold, the words from his nightmare floating through his mind.

'I'm going back to my room,' he said. 'There are one or two things I want to pick up.' Kerry smiled, rolling over onto her front.

'Nice style, Jack!' she said. 'Love 'em and leave 'em wanting more!' Giggling, she closed her eyes.

Back in his room, Jack showered and changed into a fresh set of clothes. In the lobby, he saw Kerry in a white summer dress. Her hair was tied back in a ponytail, and a pair of sunglasses perched on her forehead.

She looked at him, smiling. 'It's a beautiful morning!' she said. Jack grunted an agreement, and Kerry swung round to face him. 'That was not very chivalrous, what you did this morning.' Jack gave no response. 'A girl likes to be pampered after a night of intense passion!' Jack couldn't help but give a jocular smile.

'Intensity and passion all in the same sentence?' he said. Kerry smiled, tossing her head away from him.

'You're pushing it!'

'OK, but I needed time to think and to get a change of clothes!'

Kerry looked at him. 'And did you draw any conclusions?'

Jack shook his head. 'Only that things have got to play themselves out a bit longer. Let's go and get some breakfast.' Looking at Kerry, Jack asked, 'Do you think they are suspicious?'

'Who?'

'Égalité, Grouper or O'Reilly?'

Kerry frowned at the absurdity of Jack's question.

'Why would they be?'

'I don't know, but I feel...' He allowed his sentence to trail off.

In the restaurant, the tables were laid for breakfast; O'Reilly and Duffy were already seated. Jack spotted Grouper coming out of the kitchen. He approached them with a crooked smile. 'We'll be leaving shortly after breakfast. Mr McDuff and Miss O'Moore, you will remain here as our honoured guests. Jack and Shamus will accompany me.'

'What if I don't want to remain here?' Kerry cast Grouper a fiery and determined look, at which Grouper smiled.

'I'm afraid that you have no choice.'

Kerry rose from the table and stormed away as O'Reilly began to laugh. 'That's women for ye!' He continued to laugh as he tucked into a hearty breakfast. Jack followed Kerry, locating her by the elevators.

'What was all that about?' he asked when she turned her emerald eyes, blazing with fury.

'So I'm to be left here to twiddle my thumbs, not knowing what the hell's happening?'

'It will be for the best. I don't want to be watching your arse as well as my own! You've done your bit: you got me in. Now it's time I did mine!'

She faced him, her eyes steadfast in a mutual challenge. 'That's so typical, same attitude of the old school! Even now, when it's readily accepted that women go into combat, still that same bigoted attitude of don't put women in danger shines through your bullshit, Jack!'

Jack attempted to keep a straight face but laughed at her determined and fearless attitude. 'I can't help being "old school", as you put it.'

Kerry gave him a reproachful glance, walking into the elevator as it arrived.

When Jack returned, O'Reilly looked up, his mouth half full of food.

'Lovers' tiff?'

Jack shrugged his shoulders. 'I think she's got the hump that you and I are taking a trip.' Jack's statement brought about fresh bouts of laughter from O'Reilly.

'Pat here will keep her company while we're away.'

'I don't think she considers Pat company.' Jack's comment received raised eyebrows from Duffy and more laughter from O'Reilly.

'A bit too coarse for her, hey! Just like me!' The Irishman continued to chuckle to himself as he consumed another helping of breakfast.

The morning meal completed, Grouper escorted Jack and O'Reilly to a waiting limousine. They were taken to a small airfield and, a little later, were flown out in a small passenger plane. The sprawling metropolis below petered out to the vast expanse of plains and jungle.

The aircraft flew at a low altitude, giving a superb view of the landscape, at times, swooping so low that it disturbed herds of zebra that raced away in fright. Grouper nudged Jack. 'There is nothing like the hunt of wild game!' he said in a self-indulgent voice. 'That is, with the exception of human game. Now, that is game I truly savour!'

Jack could find no amusement in Grouper's statement and declined to answer the man, refusing to even look at him, feeling only contempt.

Flying above the Tenere Desert, the ground below was parched and arid, retaining little life. Jack felt a sickness that began in the pit of his stomach, radiating outward to encompass his entire body. He felt diseased, as something unseen gnawed at his essence. The bone-dry ravine below leaped up at him, as images stirred in his head.

He was falling backwards confronted by the spectacle of his past. He waited on the outskirts of the plains, the nomadic village before him, like a distant recollection that rode the back of a hazy dream. The drums beat a rhythmic tune, agitating the air as the scene changed, leaving the village burning, a conflagration of blazing dwellings that cavorted to the cadence of tribal drums. Out of the flames walked the boy, smiling. 'Who are you?' Jack demanded.

'You know who I am!'

Jack felt disquiet clutch at his soul. He shook his head. 'You are dead!'

'As are you!' the boy said. 'You died when I did.'

'No!' Jack screamed, denying what the boy said.

'My father brought you back with unexpected results. Look at yourself, Jack. You are slowly rotting…'

Looking down at his feet, the desert sand was replaced by water, and, as Jack peered at the surface, he saw the reflection of a corpse staring back at him. Recoiling, he looked back at the boy. 'Why?'

'Fate or chance? The evil of men, you might think. He uses the powers of nature for ill gain, a delegate of the *Djab* devils of death! He controls the passageways between the living and the dead. He is a *Bokor*, a dark voodoo priest, that holds dominion over the dead. He can and will bend you to his will!'

'Why are you telling me this? How do you know? You are dead!'

The boy smiled. 'The dead know everything, Jack. He is using you as a tool for his vengeance. Ultimately, Samdi desires power and dominion! The great *Orisha*, the four hundred spirits created by *Oludumare*, the supreme deity of the universe, stand in opposition to what he is trying to do. My mother was a gift from them to the Yoruba people as an intermediary. My father knew of her power and sought to harness it, but after she gave birth to me, she died returning to them, denying Samdi her power. So enraged was he that he attempted to reanimate her corpse. It was a disaster, but he realised she had passed that power to me, his son. So, he waited.

'Your arrival and the carnage that followed denied him even this, and now he seeks vengeance. I have been sent to stop my father's evil. He goes against everything the *Orisha* were created for!'

Jack opened his eyes. He was back in the plane, disorientated. His turmoil grew as the plane entered a steep turn, flying head-on towards a black mountain range. Scabrous pinnacles stretched across the horizon, overwhelming a green oasis beneath them. As Jack watched from the window, he viewed a scene that could have been from the beginning or the end of the world.

The mountains loomed closer, as a plateau of volcanic slag stretched out before them where a runway had been levelled allowing the aircraft to land. Jack could see there were other craft just off the runway. A small company of men awaited them on the runway. Jack observed them with a keen curiosity, as the plane taxied to a standstill.

Grouper led them from the plane and was saluted by one of the men. Jack took particular interest. They were a swarthy-looking bunch, testifying to the fact that they were fighting men.

An old battered jeep approached their position, drawing to a halt. 'They're rebels! Mercenaries and terrorists… They are the Fist of Euskadi! Come, you will see,' Grouper said, climbing into the jeep.

The vehicle carried them towards a tunnel that bore into the mountainside. Jack's attention was taken by a small group of men standing close to the entrance. One of these was Égalité. He smiled, extending his arms in an open gesture of welcome. 'Welcome, my friends!' he said as the vehicle stopped. Égalité moved away and Jack noticed Samdi, standing dutifully back. He glanced at Jack, who felt a shudder run through him.

'Welcome to the Fist of Euskadi!' Égalité said with a conceited, self-satisfied air to his voice. 'It has taken just over five years to devise and forge the dominion that you see here before you, a mere fraction in time when you consider the measure of volcanic activity that must have occurred over the many millions of years it took to create it!'

Jack now judged that the cave had once been an outlet for molten lava from the earth's core below.

'However did ye find this place in the first place?' O'Reilly asked, intrigued by the prospect of using an extinct volcano as an operational base for terrorist activities.

Égalité smiled. 'The Air Mountains called to me as I flew

across them on my way to Niamey once. It was like a voice that echoed in the recesses of my mind. "Who," it said, "would come looking for a dead man within a dead volcano?" And it was right; I have been allowed the luxury of solitude, so far away from the justice of humanity. I have an arrangement with the Touareg militia. Their presence in the area tends to keep nosy people away.'

'If we'd had a similar set up back home,' O'Reilly said, his personal thoughts rolling fluently from his tongue, 'we'd have won the fucking war!' O'Reilly's statement appeared to please Égalité.

'And you, Jack? Do you not have any observations that you wish to add?' Égalité was fishing for compliments, like a child with rich parents who subsequently had the best of everything.

Jack remained silent. Égalité appeared self-consumed with his own genius, his face becoming harsh. 'Are you impressed?' he asked, a sharp edge to his voice.

'I'll reserve judgement,' Jack said as Égalité's smile became strained, his eyes narrowing in doubt. 'What is the Fist of Euskadi? A front for gun running, or a band of mercenaries masquerading as terrorists?'

'Why all the questions, Jack?' There was a double edge to Égalité's voice; it was partly questioning, partly mistrustful.

Jack snapped at Égalité. 'Because I want to know what I'm bloody well getting myself into! You forget that I've seen the files that are related to you, and no matter how invisible you think you are, there are always people keeping tabs on you! They know that you are still alive: I've seen the evidence. Now that I've entered this house of cards – willingly, I might add – I want to determine whether it is in danger of falling down!'

Égalité tossed his head back, laughing. 'Your point is duly taken, my friend. It seems that Felix has been wise in his selection of a man such as yourself, but let me reassure you that this 'card house', as you so eloquently put it, is in no danger of falling down.'

'How can you be so sure?' Jack asked.

'I am a phantom drifting through a country of squalor and destitution: a ghost, a myth!' Jack watched, as again Égalité bathed in his own conceit. 'World governments call me a terrorist, but I am no better and no worse than they themselves are. I just operate in the underworld, the world that makes their existence possible!'

Out of the corner of his eye, Jack caught Grouper's hand resting on his gun as he listened intently to Égalité.

'In a world of capitalists, money is everything. Anything and everything is for sale – at the right price. Drugs, weapons, even people, can be bought and sold on the black market!'

Chapter 10

The cocktail lounge was half full and the sun had not yet reached its ascendancy. Duffy sat alone at one of the tables. He seemed anxious, mesmerised by the rising bubbles in the glass of beer in front of him. Kerry approached from behind.

'I wondered where you had got to!' she said, bringing Duffy out of his melancholy.

'I can't fucking move!' he snapped, in a low, but aggravated voice. Kerry was about to reply when he continued, 'Everywhere I go, I'm being bloody watched!'

'I know what you mean!' Kerry said, aware that she, too, was watched wherever she went. 'You think that they might be suspicious?' Duffy shook his head, returning to the observation of his drink.

'Suspicious, no; over bloody cautious, yes. Jack and I arranged a rendezvous at a small café in the city. But if I can't move, then I'm going to have no chance of keeping it!'

Kerry studied Duffy. As their eyes met he smiled. 'I'm not used to this. Sitting out in the bloody cold!'

The bartender approached, inquiring if they needed anything. Kerry ordered a lemonade. No more conversation passed between them until the bartender had returned with her drink and left again. Kerry's green eyes studied the man sat before her. From what she knew about Duffy, he was a loner type, a plant – probably by MI6 – intent on gathering information on the Provisional IRA, but his exact role in this situation was a complete mystery to her.

'I thought Jack was the only one that was going to be working from the inside. I mean, I thought that he was going to be the inside man.'

'So did I!' Duffy stated, taking a long draught of his beer. 'I should still be in Ireland, gathering information on gunpowder, treason and plot!' Kerry's eyes met Duffy's.

'So why are you here?' she asked. Duffy grinned, looking into the now half-empty glass.

'Victim of circumstance!' Draining his glass, he waved his hand, ordering another. He belched loudly. 'What's your excuse?'

'Same as you!' Kerry said with a coy smile. 'Victim of circumstance!'

As they moved further into the heart of the mountain, Jack became attentive. Construction was still in progress on the naturally occurring formations that penetrated down into the very heart of the extinct volcano. These labyrinthine passageways were intricate, and Jack knew he would need a more detailed layout of the terrain. He had to admit Égalité had created a perfect hideout within the mountains.

Listening to Égalité, Jack realised that the Fist of Euskadi was infinitely more dangerous than had been originally anticipated. Égalité was working to one end: to constitute himself as a force in his own right.

The passage opened out into a vast cavern. 'And this, gentlemen, is why you are here!' Égalité stated. Jack's regard fell upon two missile carriers. Riding upon their backs were two missiles.

'These, gentlemen, are what you are here to bid for: medium-range ballistic missiles that have ten times the potency of the Hiroshima bomb!' Jack felt himself go cold.

Noticing that Grouper was no longer with them, Jack looked around for him and saw him disappearing through a door marked RESTRICTED. Slipping away from the group, Jack quickly pursued him, only to be confronted by the back of a construction worker. As the man began to turn, Jack grabbed him quickly, breaking his neck. Lowering the body to the floor, Jack spotted something sticking out of his back pocket. Taking it, he saw that it was a blueprint. Then Jack stowed the body where it would not be easily found.

Back at the hotel, Jack lay on his bed, studying the construction blueprint he had taken from the worker. His mind was crowded and he felt exhausted. His eyes grew heavy. Sleep's embrace was tenacious, taking instant control. As he drifted off, he felt another presence invading his slumber. Samdi the manservant was at the forefront of his mind, portrayed as a puppet master, controlling Égalité and Grouper. The Bokor's facial features created a macabre backdrop to the spectacle.

Jack saw himself as pivotal member, working the marionettes of Samdi's mechanism. These images gnawed at his mind like wood rot at the heart of an oak tree. He tried in desperation to escape, but as he struggled against the images, another drifted into his mind. Lisa's face floated before him.

A sepulchral laughter resounded in his head, its intonation deep and maniacal.

Jack's eyes snapped open. Birds were chirping from beyond his window. He felt hollow. 'Was I asleep?' he asked himself, his voice resounding in the still room. Padding to the bathroom, he entered the shower.

The spray rejuvenated him, breaking him from the spell of sleep. There was an abrupt knock at the door. Wrapping a towel around himself, he answered it to discover Felix Grouper. The carpet at Jack's feet began to dampen as rivulets of water dripped from his wet torso.

'It seems that you are also an early riser, Jack.' Grouper's voice echoed in the confines of the corridor. 'No one else is awake yet.'

'Soldier's habits die hard!' Jack said with a smile. 'What time is it, anyway?'

'A quarter past five. Nobody else, it seems, shares our sleep patterns.'

Jack felt that there was something wrong. 'In the morning?' he asked.

Grouper gave a laugh. 'You appear to be at a loss. The jet lag of the past few days must have finally caught up with you! I was surprised that I did not see you yesterday. I checked on you but you were asleep.'

As Jack realised he'd missed an entire day, Grouper continued, 'I took it upon myself to order a fresh pot of coffee. I wasn't sure if you would be awake, but…' He let his sentence trail off as Jack picked up the remainder of the line for him.

'But you wanted to talk to me?'

Grouper nodded as Jack stepped to one side, allowing him entrance. Jack finished dressing and returned to find Grouper aimlessly looking around the room. 'So, what did you want to talk to me about?' Grouper was mindful of the question before answering.

'I want to know your thoughts, Jack! What you really think!'

'About what?'

'About Égalité! About the Fist of Euskadi!'

Jack shook his head. 'I don't understand what you mean.'

Grouper gave an enigmatic laugh, as though he viewed the world through sardonic eyes.

Jack's face remained candid. 'Well, if you want me to be frank...'

Grouper's face became a mask of deliberation. 'By all means!' he said. 'Go ahead!'

'I'm being paid not to think, or at least not to analyse.'

Grouper nodded his head, a flicker of a smile touching his lips. 'Do you want a drink, Jack? I mean a real drink!'

When Jack and Grouper entered the bar, it was illuminated softly. Walking behind the bar, Grouper selected two tumblers and placed them on the counter before him. He reached for a bottle of tequila, unscrewing the lid and pouring a liberal amount into each glass. Bringing the tumbler to his lips, he downed the content in one swift gulp. Pouring himself another, he leant heavily on the bar.

'How long have you known Égalité?' Jack asked.

'A long time, we go way back. I first met him when I was at university studying nuclear physics.' Grouper smiled. 'I had an altercation that involved a woman. There was an accident and she died, so I ran away and joined the Foreign Legion. There they taught me how to be an efficient killer...' He grinned. 'And I developed a taste for it!'

A sudden movement caused Grouper to produce a Colt .45 from beneath his jacket. Duffy ambled towards them, giving both men a cursory glance.

'Is this a private party or can anyone join?' he asked.

Grouper viewed him with distrust. 'Depends on who that someone is!' he said, in a broad South African accent. 'But as you're here, you may as well take a pew!'

Duffy cautiously approached the bar, watching Grouper as he selected another tumbler and poured a drink. Jack remained indifferent.

'Help yourself!' Grouper said, sliding the tumbler towards him. 'So, Mr McDuff! How long have you been a member of the IRA?'

Duffy reached forward and took the drink from the bar. 'Since I was ten years of age!' After taking a quantity of his drink, his eyes narrowed, locking with Grouper's. 'You don't like me much do you?' he said with a smile. 'That's OK though, because I can't say that I'm a great fan of yours! You're unpredictable and that makes you and this whole deal dangerous.'

Emptying his tumbler, he continued, 'I'll level with you now. I've advised O'Reilly to have nothing to do with this organisation. I don't know what all this is about, and I don't appreciate being left out in the cold. I just want to get the hell home!'

Grouper began to laugh, relishing the fact that he had baited the Irishman.

'If there's one thing I admire in a man, it's honesty. You may not be as bad as I had first thought, Irish. That's not going as far as to say I trust you, but you've got balls, and that's a commodity I admire!'

Duffy pushed the empty tumbler away from him. Turning his back, he walked out of the bar to the chorus of Grouper's laughter.

Grouper turned his attention back to Jack, pouring himself another drink. 'How well do you know Mr McDuff?'

'I don't,' was Jack's curt reply. He swilled tequila around the glass before knocking it back.

Grouper's eyes grew suspicious. 'You two seem to have formed a bond since we arrived here.'

Jack gave a derisive laugh. 'If you're trying to imply that we are in league together… The first time I laid eyes on the bloke was in that pub back in Ireland. Anyway, I would have thought you would have more of an insight into the man than me.' Grouper frowned. 'Weren't you with O'Reilly before I arrived on the scene? McDuff is one of his lot.' Jack shrugged his shoulders. 'Perhaps the man's lonely, and apart from O'Reilly, I'm the only one that he has anything in common with!' Jack watched as Grouper raised his eyebrows, hinting that he had gleaned some vital piece of information from his last statement.

'And what have you got in common, Jack?'

Jack smiled, seeing where Grouper intended this minor interrogation to go. 'Nothing – except we're killers from opposite sides of the divide.'

'Like minds!' Grouper said, nodding his head in agreement. 'I apologise, Jack but call me paranoid!'

'Look,' Jack said, in a sympathetic tone, 'I've no love for the Provos and I assure you that they have no love for me. Perhaps Duffy is looking to make a confederate, being in a strange country.'

'You may be right, Jack, but I don't know. There is just something about him that I don't trust. Maybe I just don't like his face!' Grouper gave a laugh.

Chapter 11

Jack spotted Kerry approaching the pool. The fabric of her dress was almost transparent, casting the outline of her figure in translucent shadow. Jack lay on a sunbed, a pair of dark glasses concealing his eyes.

'Good morning!' she said, flashing him a smile as she approached the edge of the pool. Removing her dress, she revealed a two-piece bathing suit. She gave him a brief glance before diving into the water.

Casually observing her playful antics, Jack debated whether the water looked inviting. Kerry's head and shoulders came into view above the pool rim. 'Why aren't you joining me?' she asked.

'I was thinking about it, but decided that there were too many piranhas swimming about in there!'

'I assure you there are no little fishes in this pool!'

Jack approached the edge, looking down at Kerry, her face beaded with pearls of water. Sitting on the edge, he dangled his feet in the cool water. Kerry giggled and disappeared beneath the surface, only to suddenly re-emerge, grabbing Jack's legs.

As Jack became immersed under the water, he found that it soothed his hot flesh. His head resurfaced alongside hers and he heard her say, 'It's wonderful!'

Cocking his head to one side he replied, 'You think so, do you?' and he dived, swimming underneath Kerry to grab her waist and pull her under. Jack was the first to break the surface; seconds passed as he began looking for her. He felt something brush against his feet, and he braced himself for the inevitable tug, but it never materialised. Instead, he felt soft movement slowly work its way up his body. With feather-like kisses, Kerry's head finally emerged, her eyes reaching Jack's level as she blew water in his face. She brushed his pectorals and he gently pushed her away, breaking into a breaststroke and swimming to the other end of the pool. Kerry followed him as he turned to face her.

'I've got to go into the city,' he said.

'Alone?' she asked.

As Jack looked into her eyes, he could see her longing. She kissed him gently on the corner of the mouth.

'If something should go wrong, I want you to keep a low profile, return to Ireland with O'Reilly and when you get there report what has happened to your controller.'

Kerry nodded her head somewhat reluctantly, and Jack saw that she was horrified at having to do so.

'Don't worry!' he soothed, touching her cheek and cupping it gently. 'I'm not expecting anything to go wrong!'

She displayed her disappointment by swimming away from him. Jack lifted himself out of the pool with powerful arms, the warmth of the sun signifying its presence by evaporating the moisture from his skin. Looking back at Kerry, he saw her wading in the middle of the pool, her emerald-green eyes sparkling in the sunlight, the contours of her body shimmering in the rippling water.

Duffy had been wandering aimlessly, trying to shake the tail he had acquired after leaving the hotel. He stood browsing in a shop window, using the glass's reflective properties as a mirror. There was furtive movement from his left, and a figure paused directly behind him.

Reflected in the window was the phantom image of Ferguson. His voice was unmistakable, clipped with a bogus, upper crust accent. 'Fancy seeing you here?' Ferguson mused to Duffy's back. 'You're a long way from your usual haunts!'

'Not here!' Duffy snapped, realising that this inopportune meeting could be being watched. Walking away from the window, Duffy knew that Ferguson would follow him.

Ducking down a side street, he waited for Ferguson. His wait was short-lived: not long afterwards he heard the approach of deliberate footsteps. Duffy turned to be confronted by the tall MI6 man. 'How goes it?' Ferguson asked in a mild manner.

'How did you find me?' asked Duffy.

Ferguson gave a knowing smile. 'I've been watching you since you arrived. I must say that your unexpected appearance was a surprise, to say the least. Is Jack still in one piece?'

Duffy screwed his face in a frown. 'And what is that supposed to mean?'

Again Ferguson grinned. 'Is Jack all right?'

'Yes. I think he's found a way in. Don't ask, because I don't know – I wasn't invited! I caught sight of him this morning, but it was an inopportune time for us to have a chat. Although I would say, by the look on his face, that he knows the whereabouts of the Fist of Euskadi.'

Ferguson narrowed his eyes. 'Where is Jack now?'

'I don't know! The last I saw of him, he was with Scorpion. One thing I do know for sure is that close tabs are being kept on everybody!'

'You're being watched then? How do you know that we're safe talking?'

'I lost them over an hour ago. Anyway, I've got a meet arranged with Jack. I'd say he was on his way there as we speak!'

'Good!' Ferguson thought for a long moment. 'Keep the meeting. I'll be watching!' He strode away without looking back. Something about his words and his mannerism disturbed Duffy greatly. Shrugging off the feeling, Duffy retraced his steps back to the street.

He only had an idea of where he was going; the streets were unfamiliar to him. His knowledge was confined to a briefly-detailed map of the city – the diagram was more of a sketch. What Duffy had found of relevance was that one of the street names on the map was the same as that on which Jack had told him the French café was situated.

With the information imprinted into his mind, Duffy walked the long streets of Niamey, looking for the café. Jack was crossing the road a little ahead of him. Increasing his pace slightly, Duffy caught a brief glance of him entering a building. Checking he was alone, Duffy followed him in.

He chose a table at the back of the room, sitting with his back to the wall; this way he had a view of everybody who came in. There were sounds of a belated reunion coming from the counter. Jack was engaged in playful banter with a large, robust man, who stood wearing the white apparel of a cook. The cook embraced Jack in a bear hug and kissed him once on both cheeks, his voice booming in the dining area, declaring his rapture at seeing an old friend. The man spoke with a deep French accent.

'Jacques, my friend! It has been too long!'

He gave a hearty laugh as Jack leaned across whispering something in his ear. Nodding his head, the cook disappeared into the back. Turning to Duffy, Jack said, 'We'll have more privacy in the back.'

The cook reappeared, indicating for them to follow him. Duffy found himself in a room full of ingredients stacked on the floor and on shelves. It smelt faintly of spices, and at the back of the room was a desk, illuminated by a small table lamp.

'This is Marcel,' Jack said, introducing the cook. 'He is a very old friend of mine and was once a legionnaire!' Marcel playfully slapped Jack on the arm as Duffy nodded in his direction.

'Any friend of Jacques is a friend of mine!' the big Frenchman said with an earnest smile.

In the dimly lit storeroom, Duffy felt at ease and couldn't help wondering how Jack and Marcel's friendship had been born. Since Duffy had joined the regiment, he had seen little of the world; his Irish citizenship and heritage had been exploited to the full. 'Lucky you've got friends here,' he said.

'It was by chance that I remembered Marcel. During our time we have found ourselves working in close partnership, even if our agendas were completely opposite!' Duffy watched with mild humour as the two men began to laugh at their private joke. The Frenchman spoke again.

'Well, I will leave you alone. I have a café to run!'

'You don't have to leave on our account,' Jack said.

'Whatever it is, it would be prudent that I know nothing!' As Marcel began to walk away, Jack stopped him.

'One more thing, my friend: what do you know of a fellow legionnaire called Felix Grouper?' Marcel turned slowly, his eyes containing both hate and fear.

'If I were you, my friend, I would have as little to do with him as possible. He has been AWOL from the legion for five years. The man was – how you say? – *loco*. Three legionnaires have been sent to retrieve him, all capable men – they are all dead!'

Without further conversation, Marcel left the storeroom.

In the restricted light Jack appeared pale, almost white. He faced Duffy with a worried expression 'It's not good!' he said. 'Égalité has turned the Air Mountains into a ticking time bomb!'

Duffy's face grew grave. 'Have you found the uranium?'

'Yes, and it's worse than we feared. He has two ballistic missiles, similar to the American Polaris, each loaded with a nuclear pay load.' Duffy shook his head. 'Enough to blow a sizeable hole in the Mediterranean!'

Duffy felt the cold import of the revelation seep in as Jack continued. 'If something happens to me, I want you to locate Ferguson and tell him what I've told you. He'll have to take it from there.' Jack produced the blueprint, giving it to Duffy. 'I've marked the key areas.' Duffy looked down at the map, telling Jack about his chance meeting with Ferguson.

'Ferguson was acting peculiar when I saw him. He seemed... preoccupied.'

'I shouldn't worry too much. SIS are a strange lot at the best of times,' Jack said, passing off Duffy's misgivings.

'I don't know, Jack. Maybe it's me being paranoid, but I certainly got the feeling that he was hiding something.'

A thoughtful expression crossed Jack's face. 'You said that Ferguson's been watching you since you left the hotel. So, he knows that we're here now! Why hasn't he shown himself?'

Duffy had no answer, and this inability only compounded his fears. He observed Jack with increasing concern.

Duffy watched Jack leave the storeroom, his military intuition dogging him. Everything appeared to be kosher on the outside, yet there was something he was missing. His mind kept going over his impromptu meeting with Ferguson. It was irrational, thinking that Ferguson was one of the bad guys. Yet, there was something about the agent's face, about his stance, that unnerved him.

Leaving the café, Duffy's eyes were alert. He knew he was still being tailed. He had spotted Ferguson twice from the corner of his eye. Dodging into an alley, he waited to see how observant his pursuer was. Ferguson rounded the corner.

'Have you seen Jack?'

Duffy nodded, saying, 'You know I have.'

'And…?' Ferguson's expression changed. His eyes became cold and emotionless. Duffy saw his intention too late as Ferguson drew his gun.

'Ah, ah, ah…' he jeered. 'I wouldn't do that if I were you!' He gave a winning smile, allowing Duffy time to contemplate the Heckler & Koch P7. 'You don't have to answer because I already know. Which is why I can't let you leave here alive.'

Duffy's eyes narrowed, sizing up his adversary. He sought a chink in his stance, an edge that would give him the advantage. He noted the gun's silencer, and felt anger seize him.

'You traitorous scum!' The words, spat with venomous contempt, had little effect on the agent.

'That I grant you…' Ferguson smiled. 'And if it makes you feel any better, I don't find this a very sporting task.'

Duffy felt the hatred welling within him. 'And now, I suppose, you're going to tell me why?'

'No!' was Ferguson's reply.

This was all the time Duffy needed: he lunged for the gun. Ferguson's gun arm was pushed high in the air as the two men struggled. The agent smashed his fist into his opponent's face. There were sparks before Duffy's eyes as involuntary tears blurred his vision. Shoulder-charging him, Duffy lost his footing, but he had sense enough to hold on to Ferguson, bringing the man down on top of him.

Duffy's knee connected with Ferguson's groin, and he felt his attacker go limp. Struggling with his gun arm, he managed to bring the weapon round so it was sandwiched between them.

Feeling teeth bite into his ear, Ferguson struggled to free his gun arm as both men rolled over. The shot was hardly audible, but Duffy felt the fire of hot lead as all his will to survive vanished. Rolling onto his back he coughed violently, lying motionless; his breathing was shallow. At the periphery of his vision, he saw Ferguson rise to his feet. His vision went murky and the pain grew, until all other thoughts were wiped from his mind.

Ferguson towered above Duffy's unmoving form, his gun trained at his head, his expression cold and unsympathetic. His eyes narrowed as he prepared to pull the trigger; the pool of blood swelling from the body mesmerised him. Voices not far away grew closer, and the sound of his heavy footfalls remained long after he had departed.

Chapter 12

Jack had not immediately returned to the hotel. Instead, he had chosen to wander the streets, vacantly observing the crowds around him. He viewed the distinct class divide. Scantily clad natives openly mingled with suited business people and tourists. He thought of how blissfully ignorant these people were.

As he watched, a battered, dirty bus drew to a standstill; black smoke belched from the vehicle's exhaust, indicating that a piston ring was in danger of giving way. The people who left the bus were mostly indigenous to the region, but a particular couple caught his eye. At first, Jack thought his mind was playing tricks. The man was a tall, white European and standing next to him was Lisa.

Jack was consumed with dread. All he could think was *not now,* as he glimpsed her disappear into the marketplace. He began to follow, his steps breaking into a run as he raced across the road. There was a squeal of brakes, and a horn blared loudly, but all was lost on Jack as foreboding and dread consumed him.

Barging his way through the crowd, Jack frantically searched around him, spotting them standing next to a stall. Approaching from behind, he placed his hand gently on her shoulder as she swung round, a laugh still issuing from her lips. At first, recognition was distant; then Jack saw in her eyes both shock and wonder at the same time.

'Jack!' she exclaimed, attracting the attention of the man.

Jack couldn't smile, his face remained grave and solemn.

'Jack?' she enquired. 'What are you doing here?'

Jack could find no words to utter. On other missions, he had known that his family and loved ones were safe. This situation dictated an unknown quantity. Looking bewildered, Lisa turned to her companion.

'This is Peter Strong,' she said. He looked to be around forty and extended a hand toward Jack, who glanced him up and down.

Jack's voice became serious, conveying dire implications. 'You have to get out of here! It's not safe!'

Lisa smiled, embarrassed. 'You're not making any sense, Jack.'

Holding her gently by the shoulders, he said, 'I can't go into details, but you and your friend here should take the first plane out!'

Lisa frowned, her face becoming flushed. 'But I can't! There has been an outbreak of tuberculosis in three outlying villages. We are here to offer aid. It's imperative that I – we – stay!'

'And I say that it's imperative that you leave! Something is about to go down here and I don't want you involved!'

Lisa closed her lips tight and shook her head; Jack saw the stubborn girl he had known as a teenager. Stepping backward, she placed her hands on her hips, glaring at him resolutely.

'What are you doing here, Jack? It's a long way from security work in London!'

Shrugging his shoulders, he said. 'So I lied! The work that I'm involved in you don't discuss with people.'

'Your face was plastered all over the television before I left, but your name was different.' She paused, trying to remember the name, which Jack obligingly filled in for her.

'Jacob Portello!' he said.

'That's right – they said that you murdered people!' Her eyes were both accusing and pleading that the rumours were untrue.

'You remember that last night together? When I told you that you would hear and see things about me that were not true, but I couldn't explain? Well, that's what I was talking about!'

Lisa's eyes became hard, as she stared directly into Jack's. 'So you're saying that none of it is true? And, before you answer me, how do I know you're telling the truth now?'

Jack didn't want to be drawn into a lover's tiff. 'Do you remember me telling you that I worked for a shadowy regiment within the army?'

Lisa nodded her head, the disbelieving look not leaving her eyes. 'Well, I still do! Now, if you still don't believe me, then run. Run as fast as you can, because I am a murderer like they say, and you're not safe here.'

Jack saw tears brimming in her eyes as she fell into his arms. 'Why can't you tell me the truth, Jack?'

'If I do, then I am placing you in even more danger than you are now!' His face became earnest, as he pleaded with her. 'Now please, for my sake and yours, go back where you came from!'

Jack was embroiled in the conversation and didn't see Duffy staggering towards them. He grabbed on to Lisa's shoulders before collapsing before them. Lisa screamed as Jack looked down at his comrade. Duffy looked up at him, his face ashen and fraught with pain. Then Jack saw the blood that stained the front of his shirt.

Duffy's journey had attracted the attention of many onlookers, who stood around gawking in a morbid circle. Jack bent down, gently cradling his head. His breathing was laboured, and Jack knew that he hadn't long.

Offering a weak smile, Duffy spoke in a rasping voice. 'Jack! Thank—' He began to cough; blood-stained froth bubbled at the corners of his mouth.

'Who did this to you?' Jack asked, his voice concerned and angry. Duffy's eyes began to close. Afraid that he was losing him, Jack shook him lightly, repeating his question. 'Who did this?'

Duffy's eyes opened, momentarily back in focus. 'Ferguson!' he whispered, his body going limp. Jack felt for a pulse. Realising he was dead, a frown creased Jack's brow. He checked Duffy for the map he had given him earlier. It was smeared with blood. His actions were unobserved by everyone except Lisa.

Jack remained in the background as an ambulance arrived. He watched the body being carried away, his face set in a stern resolve. Yet another fallen warrior of the brotherhood, he thought.

Lisa was rigid, her attention fixed upon the ground. Cradling her chin, Jack lifted her head. Looking into her eyes, he saw fear residing in them. 'I want you out of here! For this reason!'

Tears began to roll down Lisa's cheeks.

'Where are you staying?' he asked her.

She looked at him, her tears abating but not disappearing. 'We're booked into the Grand Hôtel du Niger. We came to the market for supplies. We were leaving for a Tomock village in the morning!'

Hugging her close to him again, Jack casually glanced across her shoulder at the crowd. 'Go there now!' he whispered in her ear. 'What number is your room?'

'296,' she replied.

'I'll be there as soon as I can! If I'm not— well, then I want you to leave as soon as possible. I'll contact you at your brother's.'

Releasing her, he lingered a moment looking at her. Then he turned and disappeared into the crowd. A moment later, Peter Strong returned to her side. 'The police would like to talk to you and that man!' he said. 'Who was he?'

'What man?' Lisa said, as she observed a uniformed policeman approaching. The policeman advanced with a very sombre look on his face. His English was not very good and he spoke with a broken French accent.

'What happened here?' he asked, as Lisa shook her head.

'I don't know!'

'The man that was with you? Where is he now?'

Lisa again shook her head. 'I don't know!' The tears had begun to roll freely from her eyes again and Peter Strong consoled her.

Kerry followed Jack from the hotel and had seen more than she had anticipated. It had been easy to tail him: Jack was not his alert self; it was as though he was preoccupied. She observed him approach a woman. They appeared to know each other, and Kerry watched, seething with jealousy, as Jack took the woman in his arms.

Duffy had come staggering out of the crowd, clutching his stomach. She had glimpsed the blood-stained shirt before he collapsed on the ground. Casting her mind back momentarily, she remembered that she was not the only one who had been observing the café. There had been another tall man who appeared to be similarly interested. He had tailed Duffy.

Watching Jack console the woman, a torrid envy fumed inside her. Who was this woman? How was she linked to Jack? And what was her purpose in the game in which they all now found themselves embroiled? Kerry had never allowed anyone to get as close to her as Jack, and her unbridled feelings went far beyond anything she had experienced before. Now there was a complication, an obstacle that was infringing on her plans and desires. She knew she was playing a highly dangerous game, and if any of her associates were to find out, her life would be in peril; but she didn't care. She was tired of the game and of the death! All she wanted – no, all she *needed* – was this one man.

Kerry watched Jack disappear into the milling crowd. When he had gone, Kerry continued to watch the woman. Intrigued to discover her identity, she decided to follow and find out exactly who and what she was.

Chapter 13

After leaving the market, Jack made his way directly back to the hotel, his mind in complete disarray. The discovery of Cameron Ferguson as a traitor posed serious complications, but the arrival of Lisa threatened to impinge on his judgement. Making his way to his room, he found that his door was wide open. Inside, Samdi confronted him. The manservant paid no great attention to Jack; he merely sat on the floor, absently dealing through a deck of cards and reshuffling them. Jack regarded him coolly when Samdi looked up, acknowledging his presence.

'I have been waiting for you, Jack!'

Jack felt anger surge through him. He needed someone to blame. 'You told them about me, didn't you?'

Samdi began to chuckle with laughter. Still shuffling the cards, he flipped them through his fingers like a card shark. It was no ordinary deck Samdi was playing with. The cards had individual pictures on them, indicating time and the moon. Jack realised that Samdi held a tarot deck.

'Why would I tell them, Jack? When you and they are serving me?'

Jack frowned, confused, as Samdi smiled, taking great delight in explaining his meaning to Jack.

'We all have to pay the reaper, Jack. Some sooner than others. You paid that price many years ago! And now you are living on borrowed time!'

Jack frowned. 'What is that? A threat?'

Samdi gave a chuckle, lightly brushing his hand across the top card of the deck. 'Do you know anything about the tarot, Jack?' he asked. When no reply was forthcoming, he shuffled the deck.

'Unlike a normal deck of fifty-two cards, the tarot is made up of seventy-eight. These cards are divided into two categories: the major and minor arcana. The major arcana are split into twenty-two cards. They represent our spiritual journey through life. The remaining fifty-six cards are the minor arcana, and they are split into four suits of fourteen cards each – the wands, the cups, the swords and the pentacles. These cards tell us about everyday events.' His attention returned to the cards in his hands. 'I wonder what the cards have in store for you, Jack?'

Single-handed, he split the deck. Laying four of the cards face down on the table, he flipped each of the cards over. Jack stared at the upturned cards.

'Here is our happy little family,' Samdi grinned, skimming his hands over the cards. Selecting the first card, he played it between his fingers. 'The Fool! This card represents Égalité, a man whose only love is money!' Skimming the card across the table, it came to rest before Jack. 'The tower!' he said, fingering the next card. 'This is the Fist of Euskadi! But a tower built without foundation is always in danger of collapsing.' Lightly touching the third card, Samdi said, 'The Devil is I, the manipulator…'

Jack's dream flooded back to him, and he was left staring at the last card. It depicted a skeletal figure clad in a hooded cloak. 'I can see you are intrigued by the last card, Jack. The Death card is you! The instrument of my ultimate revenge!'

'What do you mean?' Jack asked, his voice losing its edge.

The Bokor smiled. 'When you walked away from the village, Jack, after you had denied me my son, Grouper came back to finish the job. He slaughtered my entire village – with the exception of me!'

Jack could find only one question forming on his lips. 'Why did he leave you?'

'Because I told him to. I placed the idea in his head to take me captive. The man is a brute, an imbecile; it was not hard to plant my wishes inside that tiny, uncomprehending mind of his! He thrives on chaos, yet he hasn't the faintest idea what true chaos represents!'

'You knew beforehand that it was all going to take place?'

Samdi laughed, his eyes revealing no real mirth. 'My line goes back generations of powerful *Houngans*. Their power passed down through the years to their sons. My son too had greater power, more power than I could ever dream of, even at his tender age. You denied me any chance of harnessing that power. So you became a means to an end of my choosing... You walk the path of the dead, Jack.'

Jack was lost for words. What he heard was impossible to comprehend, but there was a conviction to Samdi's voice that made him believe resolutely.

'Loa, my son, was named after the Haitian voodoo spirits. He is – was protected by a higher order of beings that stretch back to ancient Yoruba beliefs.'

Samdi placed his hand above the Death card, mumbling a few incoherent words. Jack's attention became transfixed upon the card, watching with morbid fascination as the Death card grew in size, superimposing itself over all the others.

'This is all our fate, and it will begin with you, Jack!'

As Jack watched, his mind refused to accept what it saw. Paralysed, he thought he had been drugged somehow and this was all an induced illusion. Suddenly his limbs were free. Rapidly consumed by fear, Jack ran, Samdi's echoing laugh resounding behind him.

When Kerry arrived back at the hotel, intense emotions boiled within her. Her mind was clouded.

The sun was setting as an entourage of security greeted her. Despite her protests, she was escorted to the elevator and taken to Égalité's private suite. Standing in the open doorway to what amounted to a plush conference room, she looked at those assembled: Égalité, O'Reilly and Grouper. She didn't see Jack, and she instantly knew that was what this was about. There was also someone else present in the room, and she recognised him as the man that had followed Duffy. Scrutinising the faces before her, she sensed a mounting tension.

Égalité stood at the head of a large table, but all eyes were focused upon her. She watched Égalité turn his back when Grouper rose from his seat, grabbing her by the arm. Struggling, she tried to protest but was silenced by the look of aversion on Grouper's face. As he marched her to the table, Égalité casually turned round, holding a glass of champagne. He scrutinised her, and when he spoke it was in an authoritative tone.

'It appears that your boyfriend, lover, or however you wish to describe him, is not wholly what he seems!' There was a smoothness to Égalité that made Kerry feel sick. Dabbing at the corners of his mouth with a napkin, he paused, allowing Kerry time to think about what he had said. She shifted uncomfortably, but Grouper's grip on her arm was excessively tight. 'So what we would like to know is, exactly who is he?'

Kerry saw from Égalité's eyes that he already knew the answer. Yet Kerry maintained a defiant stance. 'He's Jacob Portello!' she stated categorically.

'Are you telling the truth?' Égalité asked. 'You see, I already know the truth. The whole truth, that is. Mr Ferguson here' – he nodded towards the stranger seated at the table – 'has filled me in, so to say. Particularly the details about you, Miss O'Moore. Or should I call you Scorpion?'

'His name is Jacob Portello!' Kerry stated again, feeling uncomfortable. Her eyes flicked from Égalité to O'Reilly, who sat with a thunderous expression on his face, the small veins on his cheeks prominent. His eyes filled with hate.

'Do you know what I do with traitors, Miss O'Moore?' Kerry's attention was drawn back to Égalité.

There was an ominous atmosphere in the room. Ferguson's abrupt laughing shattered the deathly silence, and all eyes turned in his direction. He spoke in a clear and unruffled voice. 'If I could just stop you a moment, Phillip. I did say that Miss O'Moore was working for us, but...' He directed his attention to Kerry. 'That is not strictly true, is it, Miss O'Moore?'

Kerry felt the blood in her veins freeze, a dark cloud descending upon her. She couldn't speak.

'Miss O'Moore has made a fine show of things, being a dedicated army operative. When I discovered her involvement in the mission, I decided to do one or two checks of my own. My research laid bare facts that are rather interesting. Kerry O'Moore is a living lie, a double agent for the Provisional IRA! Isn't that so, Kerry?' Kerry saw O'Reilly smile. 'Her orders were to find out as much as possible about you, Mr O'Reilly, but she has been working for you the whole time!' Ferguson's eyes rested on the smirking Irishman.

O'Reilly stared back at Ferguson. 'Ye told us that Kerry was working for the British, that you had concrete proof of this! Now ye are telling us what I already knew! What I'd like to know, Mr Ferguson, is what's in this for you? I mean, ye've made a point of embarrassing Kerry here, but what about ye? Ye've changed ye colours once. What's to say ye won't do it again?'

Ferguson glared at the Irishman, when Égalité turned his smooth and beguiling attention on him. 'It has been some months now since you came to me and informed us of your government's intentions, but it appears that you have not told me everything. I do not like games, Mr Ferguson, and I don't like people who play them with me!'

As an agent Ferguson had watched others around him rise into elevated positions, command greater salaries with comfortable office positions. He was a ground man who had to find a way to keep ahead of the game. He had always provided his paymasters with what they wanted, but only just. Choice bits of information he kept to himself, selling it to keep him in a comfortable lifestyle.

There was a moment's hesitation and Égalité detected it, smiling knowingly. 'But surely, Mr Ferguson, you don't think I do business with just anybody. I check them out! You, for instance, appear to be a typical case of hard done by and over-looked. Your controllers seem to think you are a capable individual, but not an exemplary one. It is always better to be aware of one's enemies than not. Don't you agree?'

Ferguson defended himself. 'What are you trying to imply?'

Grouper answered with scorn. 'What he is implying is that a traitor can be used but never trusted!'

'OK. I need a way out. I thought that if I did a deal with you, then it would provide my train ticket!'

Égalité studied Ferguson. The agent tried to maintain his calm. 'You don't get to where I am today by trust. It's a commodity I can't afford, though I admire it. So the question is, am I going to trust you?' Ferguson felt that the game was up. His life balanced on a knife edge. 'I will, however, honour our agreement – so long as you're useful!'

Ferguson felt relief and fear at the veiled threat, as Égalité returned his attention to Kerry. 'So it seems, Miss O'Moore, that you are indeed comrades-in-arms of sorts. The problem does, however, remain as to the whereabouts of Jacob Portello – or should I say, Jack Hornsby!'

'I'll find him,' Grouper said. 'Mr McDuff as well!'

'McDuff is dead!' Ferguson snarled.

Kerry needed to make good the situation. 'Something you may not know is that Duffy got to Jack before he died!'

Égalité became concerned. 'How do you know this?'

'Because I followed Jack to a meeting he had arranged with McDuff. After the meeting, Jack went to the marketplace where he met someone else – a woman and a man.'

Ferguson looked worried. 'Who were they?' he asked.

'I don't know. The woman seemed to be surprised to see him. Then McDuff appeared.'

'Did they say anything to each other?' Ferguson asked.

Kerry nodded. 'They spoke briefly.'

Ferguson's expression grew grave as Grouper laughed.

'Where did Jack go?' Égalité enquired. Kerry felt like she had committed a cardinal sin, the true motives of her betrayal laid bare before her.

'Jack was headed back here, I think. I followed the woman.'

'And where did she go?' Égalité pressed.

'She went to a hotel on the east side of the city.'

Égalité smiled in triumph. 'Then we have somewhere to begin.' He turned to Grouper. 'Bring her to me!'

Outside the boardroom Kerry turned on Ferguson, her face flushed with fury. 'I don't know what your game is!' she snapped.

Ferguson simply smiled. 'We are all friends here now, Kerry.' There was a derisive tone to his voice. 'If our mutual cooperation is to work for the benefit of all, then we have to bury our mistrust!'

Kerry eyed him coldly. 'To trust the enemy is to invite a viper into one's home! You've sold out your fellow countrymen. Whatever the rights and wrongs, you can never trust a turncoat, and I for one never will!'

Kerry's eyes flared with anger as Ferguson replied, 'Who are you to be slinging recriminations around? Aren't you selling out all your friends in England? Aren't you selling out the memory of your mother, your English mother?'

Kerry spat in Ferguson's face as O'Reilly stepped to her side.

'Be careful!' he warned. 'Kerry has sold out no one. She knows where her roots and allegiances lie!'

Ferguson gave a dry chuckle. 'Is that so?' he said, walking past them both. 'Is that so?'

Jack's mind was in turmoil. So many things were happening at the same time, he could think about it no more. His main priority was to get the information back to the Colonel. The revelation that Ferguson was a traitor had strengthened his resolve. He resolutely refused to think about Samdi and what he had said, but it nagged at the back of his mind.

He could not return to the hotel. Ferguson's involvement changed things; his cover had been blown wide open. He had to call in an old favour from a friend who worked at the British Embassy.

His mind focused, Jack hailed a taxi, giving the driver his destination. The taxi drew to a standstill outside the British Embassy. Jack climbed out under the suspicious observation of the Embassy guards. The gates were closed and two sentries stood either side inside the perimeter. They tightened the grip on their weapons as Jack approached. 'Halt!' a voice shouted. 'Don't come any closer! State your business!'

Jack froze. 'My name is Jack Hornsby. Sergeant Hornsby of the 22nd Special Air Service. It is imperative that I speak to William Norton. He is the first aide to the Ambassador.'

'You're a little out of touch,' the guard said. 'William Norton has not worked here in over two years.'

Jack became despondent on hearing the news. 'Can I see the Ambassador?'

'Sorry, sir,' the second guard said, 'but the Ambassador only sees people by appointment.'

Jack knew that there was absolutely no chance that he was going to get in. The guards were trained professionals. He used a pass phrase that he had been told to use in an emergency when he was part of the Regiment.

'The March hare is leading the parade!'

This was a priority code meaning danger. The two soldiers looked at each other briefly before unlocking the gates, their weapons trained and safeties off.

'You'd better come inside,' the first sentry said, as Jack stepped through the gates. 'You're not to move!' the soldier commanded.

'Tell them to contact Colonel Windburn at Hereford headquarters and use the code name Trooper!'

The soldier disappeared while his comrade remained with Jack, his face cast in stone. Jack watched the first soldier on the telephone. He waved, indicating for his partner to lower his weapon. 'It's OK!' he said, looking at Jack. 'Well, Trooper, it seems that the Ambassador wishes to see you.'

Jack gave a slight nod of his head and was escorted into the Embassy building. The Embassy itself was reminiscent of the Victorian era, adorned with creature comforts of a bygone age. Sweeping stairs led up to the first floor, the marble floor a patchwork of black and white, resembling a large chessboard. A door opened, and a man in a plain grey flannel suit appeared. The man was as plain in face as he was in dress; as he approached, he scrutinised Jack. 'If you would follow me, please!' he stated walking towards the staircase, leaving Jack to follow.

The stairs finished on a balcony with oak doors closed at either end. Jack's guide knocked once on the door to the right, entering. Left alone, Jack pondered a row of bookshelves, perusing a few of the titles.

He was startled by the grey man loudly clearing his throat. 'If you don't mind? It is this way.'

Jack found himself in a room that had been laid with a plush Persian carpet; bookshelves ran the entire perimeter of the room. At the far end was a squat, bespectacled man seated behind a large desk which dwarfed him in comparison. He looked up, smiling congenially, observing Jack from behind the rim of his spectacles. Rising from his seat, he stepped forward with an outstretched hand.

'Jack, it's good to see you! It has been too long!' A wide, beaming smile spread across the Ambassador's face. 'I must say that this is an unexpected and surprising visit. Code name Trooper! It's all a bit dramatic isn't it?'

'Hello, sir!'

'Come now, Jack, I thought we were past the formalities years ago!'

'I'm sorry, Roger, but time is imperative, and I have certain information that has to be passed back to Hereford urgently!'

'It sounds a bit cloak and dagger!' the Ambassador said.

'It's a long story, and one I wouldn't like to get into here. I'm pressed for time. I'm asking for a secure line to Hereford.' The Ambassador knew not to ask too many questions. 'I have a friend who is staying at the Grand Hôtel du Niger. I want you to put her on the first available flight back to the UK.'

Sitting down, the Ambassador placed his hands behind his head. He was deep in thought. 'Is it safe to say that this friend of yours may be in some sort of danger?' he asked.

'Yes and no. Let's just say that to be on the safe side, I would prefer it if she was well out of harm's way!'

The Ambassador looked concerned. 'I don't want to disillusion you, but the airport will be closed for the next thirty-six hours. A bomb scare has put a halt to all outbound and incoming flights. As you feel so strongly about your friend, I can arrange to have her stay here for a while.'

Jack felt despondency tug at him. 'If it helps,' he continued, 'then you may stay here as well!'

Grouper viewed the front of the Grand Hôtel du Niger through a pair of high-focus binoculars. Occupying the top floor of a nearby building, he watched a diplomatic car draw to a standstill outside the main doors of the hotel and observed Jack leave the vehicle. Kerry stood behind him and he could sense her unease. He liked fear and inhaled deeply, breathing in Kerry's musk.

'You like him?' he asked in a deep and monotonous voice, shattering the mood around them.

'Like who?' Kerry asked, her voice faltering. Grouper smiled at her dilemma. Betraying her country was one thing, but delivering her lover at the same time would leave mental scars that would last for life.

'Jack!' he replied. 'You seemed divided about giving him up back there.' He prepared to open her wounded heart a little further. 'You realise that you have signed his death warrant. But then it's better him than you, eh?' Grouper grinned as she turned her back on him. 'I liked him, too!' he said. 'I could sense that death followed him. When you kill a man, the darkness of the act permeates your soul. I can see that darkness.'

Turning round, Grouper said, 'You don't know whether to kill him or kiss him, do you?' He gave a humourless laugh. 'When he is dead, your revenge will feel more final.'

'I didn't want it to come to this!' Kerry said.

Grouper laughed. 'It all comes to this in the end!'

'Quite the philosopher, aren't we?' she snapped. Grouper, observing the anger flaring in her emerald eyes, licked his lips, imagining all the things he would like to do to her. How he would relish making her scream!

Catching that glint in his eye, Kerry hardened her resolve. She wished that Jack would kill him and that other psychopath, Égalité. She wanted Jack to wipe them away and sweep her off her feet, but harsh realities had taught her that life was nothing more than survival, and what she was doing now was the only way to survive.

Returning his attention to his surveillance, Grouper asked, 'What does this woman look like?'

Kerry paused before answering, questioning her own motives. 'Early to mid-twenties,' she said. 'Brunette with shoulder-length hair, small and very attractive. I'm sure you won't miss her! Model material, sort of stands out in the crowd!' Kerry despised herself; she could hear the envy creeping back into her voice and knew that Grouper could hear it too. He removed himself from the window as Kerry asked, 'Where are you going?'

Grouper stopped mid stride. 'Across to the hotel. Lover boy's just arrived!' He grinned, seeing the pain in Kerry's eyes.

Taking no chances, Grouper kept a tight hold of Kerry's arm. 'Smile!' he said through gritted teeth. To the casual observer it appeared as if the two were lovers, his large arm tightly draped across her shoulders.

As they entered the hotel, Grouper surveyed the lobby. They were alone except for a man dressed in a red jacket standing behind the reception desk. He smiled congenially as they approached.

'Can I be of assistance?' he enquired.

'Yes,' Grouper replied. 'We are looking for a gentleman by the name of Portello.' The desk clerk quickly scanned a book before him.

'We don't appear to have anyone of that name in residence at the moment. Are you sure you have the right hotel?'

Kerry observed the clerk's eyes; he was getting suspicious. 'Oh, forgive us!' she giggled. 'The gentleman he is referring to has just entered the building. He's not a guest here, but I believe he is visiting a friend. He may have used the name Hornsby.'

'A tall man,' Grouper cut in. 'With a scar down his cheek.'

'Ah, you must be referring to the gentleman friend of Miss Dempsey…' The clerk stopped himself short. Regaining his composure, suspicion grew in the clerk's eyes as he said, 'I will inform them that you are here!'

As he reached for a telephone, Grouper lunged forward with one of his large paws, clamping down on top of the clerk's hand. In a single movement, the clerk was lifted up and pulled over the reception desk. He landed heavily at Grouper's feet. Raising his large, booted foot, Grouper stamped on the clerk's windpipe, whipping his heel round until he heard a snap. Kerry watched in horror as Grouper reached over the counter, grabbing the ledger. He scanned the contents, dropping the book on the dead clerk. 'Room 296!' he said, before moving the dead clerk's body out of sight.

Kerry tried to evaluate Grouper as he dragged her with him; the man's face was bullish, but something resided in his eyes. For all his hideous appearance, Grouper had laughing eyes that mocked the world around him. He moved with a deliberate gait, his pace slowing as they approached the door of room 296. Unholstering a 9 mm Beretta, he checked that the weapon was loaded. Glancing at Kerry, he knocked on the door.

It had been surprisingly easy for Jack to persuade Lisa to accompany him to the Embassy, but persuading Peter Strong had been a different matter. Jack could see the wanton desire in the other man's eyes when he first met him. Peter had maintained that he was adequate protection for Lisa, and the only real protection she needed was from the likes of criminals like him, Jacob Portello.

'Oh, I've had you checked out. I know all about you, Jacob Portello. I didn't like the look of you when I first saw you, and Interpol have been informed of your whereabouts!' he told him.

Jack had grasped the man by both lapels. 'If you know so much about me, then you know I'm not to be crossed. But it's lucky for you that Jacob Portello doesn't exist, because he wouldn't think twice about wiping you out!'

Jack sat thinking about the stubbornness of the man, when there was a sudden knock at the door. Jack rose from his seat, leaving Lisa to finish packing. 'Can't he get it through his thick head?' Jack said, opening the door.

'Hello, Jack!' Grouper sneered, firing a single bullet into his leg. The searing pain sent Jack down, and Grouper stepped over him. Jack shouted for Lisa to run. It was a futile effort, he knew – where could she go? – but it could buy him precious seconds.

Lisa stood in the open doorway of the bathroom, confused and frightened. She was rooted to the spot, staring at a man with a gun pointed at her. 'You move,' Grouper said with heavily accented English, 'and you're dead!'

Jack tried to get up, but the big man turned round, placing his foot in the small of Jack's back. 'You take her!' Grouper snapped, when a second person entered the room. Jack caught a glimpse of the legs, and instantly knew they belonged to Kerry. The offending foot removed, Jack was rolled over, allowing him to see Grouper's hideous face. 'Lights out, Jack!' he said, swiftly delivering a kick to his jaw. 'Bring her!' Grouper stated, scooping Jack up off the floor and throwing him across his shoulder. Kerry took Lisa by the arm, finding little resistance in her.

Jack woke with a groan, totally unaware of his surroundings. His vision was unfocused, blurred at the edges, like looking through a milk bottle. His head pounded, and he couldn't feel his hands or feet. Where am I? was the first thought that entered his mind. Harsh blows rained down on his face. He was vaguely aware that someone was speaking.

On another level, he heard the words spoken by Samdi. 'You're already dead, Jack!' echoed through his mind.

The cruel and harsh coldness of ice water in his face served as a rapid reviver. Jack tried to force his eyes open. The light blinded him, filling his vision with an unnatural glare. A face hovered before him, the glare temporarily blocked from his eyes. The iridescent glow gave the face a semblance of a halo, but Jack knew that this was no angel sent to his rescue. The face belonged to Phillip Égalité.

'At last, you are with us, Jack!' he stated in a cold voice. Égalité began to shake his head, smiling as if berating a child. 'Did you really think you could get away with it, Jack? And to what end, I ask myself. So, you are going to answer a few of my questions!'

Jack's top lip curled in a snarl. 'I won't answer anything!'

Again a cruel laugh came from Égalité. 'I have many instruments of torture. Given time, any one of them would force a confession from you, Mr Portello. Or should I call you Hornsby? Jack Hornsby, formerly of the British SAS!'

Égalité's revelation came as no great surprise to Jack. He offered no reply.

'But who are you working for now?' The question was thrown into the air, and Égalité neither waited for nor expected an answer.

'Your silence is reassuring, and I know that your pain tolerance level is extremely high, which means that we could be here for days, if not weeks. Eventually you would break – this I am sure of – but the problem that faces me now is time. There are drugs that I could administer but, to be honest, I am unsure of their effectiveness. I believe that they affect the mind, making the subject tell his interrogator exactly what he wants to know. Whether this is fact or fiction I do not know, but I find that the heart can be where most people's weaknesses lie. I am, of course, talking about matters of the heart, as opposed to the physical heart!'

Suddenly the bright light that had been trained in Jack's eyes blinked into non-existence. Jack found himself facing a black perspex screen. The dark, reflective surface lifted like a veil, and Jack peered into a white and clinical-looking room. His eyes immediately alighted upon Lisa, whom he could see tied to a chair. Her face was bruised and battered, and Jack let out a shrill cry of defiance. Lisa sat motionless, her head slumped forward, as

Jack tore his eyes away. In the centre of the room was a large wooden piece of apparatus that bore a big and wicked-looking blade at its summit. The guillotine was primed, with its heavy blade ready to drop at the movement of a lever. His eyes blurring with tears, Jack looked at Lisa. He knew she was not dead; there was a distinct rise and fall to her body as she continued to breathe.

'You bastard!' Jack spat the words at Égalité.

'I see now that I have gained your full and undivided attention. You see, there is no better way to gain a person's regard than to allow them to observe a loved one's peril!'

'Let her go, Égalité! She has nothing to do with this!'

Égalité smiled. 'So it has become apparent, but I am afraid at this late stage things have gone too far. As I am sure you are aware, Mr Grouper has a somewhat overzealous tendency as regards women. If it is of any comfort, I can assure you he has been more subdued with Miss Dempsey!'

Jack let his anger explode. 'What the hell do you want?'

There was a short silence before Égalité replied.

'I will promise you one thing: your death will be quick! As to that of Miss Dempsey's… Well, let us say: that will reside entirely with you.'

'I despise you!' Jack spat. 'And all people like you! It's not so much the fact that you profit out of other people's misery; it's that you crave and thrive on that misery. People like you should be put down!'

Égalité applauded Jack's speech. 'Bravo!' he commended. 'Your resilience is admirable and quite true, I might add. But what this is really about is money.'

Jack watched a door open into the room as Grouper entered. He wore a smile of perverse contentment as he approached Lisa. Jack's eyes narrowed, feeling anger and rage.

'I hope you are awake, Jack! I'm afraid you have missed most of the fun, but I'm sure you don't want to miss the final act!' Grouper's voice drifted out on speakers that were beyond Jack's range of vision. Flexing his hands, Jack tried to work the bonds free.

'I will ask you this only once! Whom have you told?' Égalité asked.

'No one!' Jack said with contempt.

'How do I know you are telling the truth?' Égalité said. Jack watched, mesmerised, as Grouper lifted Lisa from the chair, carrying her to the guillotine. Putting her down, he positioned her head directly beneath the blade. After securing her hands and feet, he looked at the lever. Grouper's mind began to conjure images of inserting himself into her as the blade descended, striking home with a hollow *thunk*. If he had been on his own, then that would have been exactly how events would have occurred, but with the addition of an audience Grouper had to curtail his more colourful desires. The performance of his more sickening acts was taboo in the presence of Égalité. Besides, Grouper had his time with the girl where he had acted on his base desires. Still, he could not resist the urge to place his hand on her rump.

'I have to commend you, Jack…' Égalité continued. 'You are a very resourceful man! You single-handedly infiltrated our organisation!'

Shifting his gaze momentarily, Jack looked at Égalité.

'I'm a one-off actor! I haven't got time to learn lines. Improvisation is the key to my success.'

'Success being the operative word, but in the past tense. It seems that your improvisation let you down this time. Now, let us return to the matter in hand. I grow weary of your word games, Jack! Felix!' Égalité spoke loud with a commanding voice, and Jack watched as Felix produced a lighter and flicked at the wheel, instantly igniting a flame. He moved the lighter closer to Lisa.

'Stop!' Jack said. 'I told you that I told no one. The man I was supposed to report to obviously works for you, so the rest you already know!'

Jack watched in a detached way as Égalité reached into his tuxedo pocket; he knew he was going for a gun. Égalité nodded his head, and Jack flinched as Grouper released the blade. Jack heard rather than saw the blade strike home.

Letting loose a shout of defiance, his muscles strained and swelled against his restraints. Jack turned his head briefly, glimpsing the people present at his execution. It was like the dream. There were four of them: O'Reilly, Égalité, Kerry and

Ferguson. Jack's lip curled as he bared his teeth, a long, shrill sound escaping him. There was someone else standing in the shadows, and, drifting through the air, unheard by anyone else, was a low laughter: the laughter of Samdi the *Bokor*. 'Soon you will be mine, Jack. Very, very soon!'

Jack felt his bonds loosen; all rational thought was denied him. All he felt was a consummate rage.

Watching with an apathetic mien, Égalité raised his gun and fired three shots, each one striking Jack's heart.

Jack was floating, looking down on his now useless and defunct body. He was free of all mortal cares as he heard Samdi say, 'The Death card is you, Jack. Now you are mine!'

Chapter 14

Felix Grouper stood leering over Jack's corpse. 'Goodbye, Jack!'

He nudged the corpse with his foot as Égalité addressed Ferguson.

'Are you sure that no word got through?'

Ferguson shook his head. 'Last time I was in contact with HQ was approximately three hours ago. They told me that they had received no word from Hornsby, and that I should keep closer tabs on my field operatives.'

'And are you as confident about Mr McDuff?'

Ferguson smiled smugly. 'Apart from the exchange he had with Hornsby in the marketplace, Duffy had no opportunity to contact anyone except me!'

Grouper scrutinised Ferguson with distrust. He was too oily, too slippery around the edges. The man had no loyalties to anyone other than himself.

'Does this distress you, my dear?' Égalité asked Kerry as she stared down at Jack's lifeless form. As she turned away from the body, Grouper gave a gruff chuckle and Égalité's regard fell on him. 'Dispose of it!' he ordered.

As the room emptied, silence purged the atmosphere. Basking in the solitude, Grouper released Jack's restraints. Looking down upon the lifeless corpse, he said, 'It's just you and me now, Jackie boy.' He was irritated that Jack's eyes were closed. He savoured looking a corpse in the eye – it felt like he was challenging death itself. At the sudden approach of two men, Grouper looked up. Standing to attention, the men awaited their orders. 'Where have you been?' Grouper growled. 'Clean this up!' Both men offered no comment, simply moved towards Jack's body, taking hold of the shoulders and legs.

They dropped the body heavily to the ground. Producing a cigarette, the taller of the men offered one to his companion. 'I wouldn't like to get on the wrong side of Felix Grouper! Would you, Harper?' His statement contained respect, and there was a little bit of awe in his voice. His companion, a white Corsican male with the beginnings of a rough beard, shook his head.

'I've seen dozens like him, Finney, too stuck up his own arse to see the light at the end of the tunnel. He's ex-special ops. Thinks he's a hard bastard!'

The two men began to laugh, dragging the corpse behind them.

After they had collected the other corpse, Finney commented, 'Nice body, shame about the head!' He laughed at his own joke.

Harper found no mirth in the comment. Things felt weird, and he didn't like it. 'Let's just get this over with!'

Both men climbed aboard an American Cherokee jeep, Finney dragging deeply on a cigarette.

'Fucked if I know why we have to travel all the way out to the Djado plateau to dispose of the bodies. I don't know why we can't just burn them like we usually do, or just leave them in the desert for the vultures to pick clean.'

'They were Mr Égalité's precise orders!'

The vehicle's headlights cut a swath through the all-consuming darkness; the stars were the only points of reference that the two men had, and they were driving by instinct and a compass. No road lined the way to their intended destination.

'This is going to be an all-nighter!' Finney said.

Harper drove in silence. Something was disturbing him. Whether it was something he had eaten or the mood of the desert, he couldn't quite put his finger on, but it left him with an obscure feeling emanating from his stomach. There was something weird going on. It crept up behind like an unseen and stalking presence. The further he drove into the unending darkness, the more this abnormal sensation descended upon him. It was like being watched. Scanning the darkness, he felt someone, or something, was out there, tracking their progress.

Harper's nerves were on edge, and when Finney suddenly coughed he nearly left the driving seat. 'What's up with you?' Finney asked, sensing Harper's unease.

Finney saw tiny beads of perspiration on Harper's brow;

Harper shook his head, shaking away sweat that was running into his eyes.

'Nothing!' he mumbled, becoming angry with himself for his overwrought foolishness. Finney asked no more questions, seeming to accept his answer.

After driving for hours, they finally came upon the plateau. The headlights picked out the outline of a ruined village. 'We're here!' Harper said.

Stopping the vehicle, Harper's feelings of apprehension came rushing back. Unsubstantial light shone down from above, recreating the ruined dwellings of the village as macabre obelisks that beckoned with dark intent.

Climbing out of the jeep, both men grabbed shovels from the back of the vehicle. Jack's lifeless arm shifted its position, gravity working its own kind of magic upon the corpse.

'Let's do it!' Finney said. Harper simply nodded his head.

They found the ground unyielding to their labour; it was compact and impenetrable, the sand consolidated by a relentless sun during the day, and frozen hard during the sub-temperatures at night. The work was hard and relentless, but after hours of labouring they finally succeeded in hollowing a shallow furrow, which they decided would be sufficient for both of the bodies.

Laid side by side, the two corpses resembled lovers in a deathly and ghastly embrace. Jack's arm was loosely draped across Lisa's shoulders, her head lying face down and a few inches away from her neck.

As Harper and Finney began the arduous task of covering the corpses, a biting wind began to blow, carrying sand particles that chaffed against their skin and whispers of the dead rode upon the currents of air, foretelling doom.

Both men, exhausted by their task, limped sore and exposed back to the jeep. Harper stopped listening. 'Can you hear that?'

'Hear what?'

'It's like singing.'

'It's the wind, old son. Next you'll be telling me that Lawrence of Arabia has come to lend us a bloody hand.'

As they climbed into the jeep, the barely audible chant lulled them into an encroaching sleep.

Kerry stood alone with her back pushed firmly against the door, her arms enfolded around herself in a tight embrace. Shaking, tears moistened her cheeks. She was afraid, but this was nothing compared to her shame. Kerry hadn't wanted to be brought to the Air Mountains; she hadn't wanted to become any more involved than she already was.

Two deaths now hung heavily on her mind, and she wrestled between her convictions and her shame. She felt the door being pushed. Quickly, she wiped her eyes.

The door swung open, but Kerry did not turn to see who entered. A familiar smell alerted her senses. O'Reilly's stench was unmistakable; Irish whisky tinged with Old Spice aftershave and body odour. He placed a comforting arm around her shoulders, guiding her round to face him.

'Why the tears?' he asked.

Kerry couldn't look him in the eye, as fresh bouts of tears erupted. She remained silent, but to O'Reilly she didn't have to say a word. He had seen how attached the girl had become to the British bastard. On many occasions in the past, O'Reilly had used Kerry to impart some information to the British when one of his counterparts had stepped out of line, or when he had wanted to dispense with a rival. So he was as much a traitor to his cause as Jack and Kerry were to theirs.

'What's the matter, girl? Surely you're not getting so emotional about a Brit?'

He watched her eyes narrow. 'For all he was,' she said, 'I couldn't help but be drawn towards him!'

Looking into her face, O'Reilly observed that her make-up was all smudged. 'Aye, he was a handsome devil in a knavish sort of way, but a Brit and a traitor to boot!'

Kerry's face dropped a little. 'And the girl? Did Égalité have to go to such dramatic effect on the girl?'

O'Reilly's face became weary and downcast. He had been present at many a beating and had carried out a few executions in his time, but the one thing O'Reilly had never done was prolong death. He had not committed the iniquitous act of torture.

'Is it remorse you're feeling? Is that why you're acting the way ye are? Because you delivered not only Jack, but also the woman into their hands?'

Kerry averted her gaze, trying to turn her back upon the truth, as thought her denial of the remark would make the truth disappear altogether.

O'Reilly saw the discomfort his words had caused, instantly regretting what he had said. God, I need a drink, he thought, as Grouper strode into the room. He wore a pallid expression that Kerry found chilling.

'Mr Égalité wishes to see you,' he stated. Kerry exchanged a glance with O'Reilly, conveying an unspoken message. O'Reilly, too, felt like he had entered the jaws of a dragon.

'We will be along in a moment!' O'Reilly answered, his brisk and powerful Irish brogue suddenly becoming weak and insubstantial. Back in Ireland he had been a big fish in a small pond, but here, in this arid hell-land he was nothing, a minion at the beck and call of Égalité.

'He does not like waiting!' Grouper stated with a sneer.

'I don't take kindly to following orders, Mr Grouper! It is normally I who give them!'

Grouper turned as O'Reilly looked upon his back. He sensed that the big man was smiling and watched as he shrugged his broad shoulders.

'Then you have a lot to learn O'Reilly. But have it your way! I wouldn't leave it too long though.'

O'Reilly remained steadfast, staring at the big man's back as he walked away. Looking at Kerry, he asked, 'He scares you doesn't he?'

'He makes my skin crawl!' she said.

'Well, we had better go and see what Égalité wants before he sends the maniac back!'

Kerry shuddered at the thought.

Colonel Oliver Windburn stared at the sheet of paper before him. It had been neatly written by hand in a format that was universally understood. The Colonel disliked typewritten reports: although neat in structure they reflected very little about the person who had written them. Colonel Windburn insisted that all reports that crossed his desk were to be handwritten.

The style of this particular report he knew well. His personal secretary had written it and he was comfortable with her style, but the tale the report told was something of the utmost concern to the Colonel and possibly the entire world.

What pressed most was the fact that a small terrorist organisation was a front for a global weapons distribution and terrorist-for-hire network. If Jack's evaluation was correct, then the Fist of Euskadi was a producer of and merchant to the terrorist and criminal world. The report also confirmed that the uranium was still in the hands of Phillip Égalité.

Putting his fears and deliberations temporarily to the back of his mind, Colonel Windburn began to formulate a contingency plan. The report had been received an hour ago, directly from the British Embassy in Niger. The statement that Cameron Ferguson was a traitor disturbed Colonel Windburn greatly, but the report also confirmed that he had made the correct choice in using Jack.

He was pained to discover that Corporal Duff was dead. Jack's words, although not written by his own hand, told of a grievous network of deceit and betrayal that had been injected into the British intelligence network. It was imperative that he handle this information with the utmost care. Government had to be informed. Reaching forward, he picked up the telephone. 'Get me the Minister of Defence!' he said. 'Then tell Captain Harrington that Operation Trooper is go!'

The SAS officer arrived as the Colonel finished speaking with the Minister on the telephone.

'You've been briefed?' the Colonel asked, looking up at Graham Harrington.

'Not yet.'

The Colonel's face was grave. 'Well, this is how it stands. The Air Mountains in Niger have been transformed into an illicit base of operations for the Fist of Euskadi. Jack contacted us just over an hour ago providing plans of a subterranean complex, which is housed within the mountains themselves. He has confirmed our worst fears: that the uranium is arming two ballistic missiles. Retrieval of the uranium is now of the utmost importance. We can't allow the material to fall into the wrong hands. In a worst-case scenario you are to render the missiles useless – by methods being worked on as we speak. Any questions?' The Captain shook his head. 'Good! How's your French, Graham?'

Harrington smiled. 'Fine.'

The Colonel, however, did not share Harrington's mirth.

'Good, because you may be going in as French Legionnaires and not as British soldiers. Is your squadron assembled?'

'Yes.'

'You can expect some heavy resistance, so I want no heroics. Just in and out, do you understand?'

Harrington nodded his head. 'Yes, sir.

Chapter 15

It awoke from an abhorrent nightmare cold and empty; devoid of emotion and feeling, consumed by the hollowness it felt. A clawed hand broke free of the loose earth, the rest of its upper torso following. Sitting up, the corpse looked upon the world, disjointed from its surroundings. Nothing existed except a basic need to kill.

Everything it saw was a vague impression imprinted upon it. The world around ebbed with an infinite luminosity that swelled from the very sand itself. A memory flickered at the edge of recollection.

Desire took over when it spotted movement on the ground. A snake slithered in close proximity to the corpse's hand. The West African Carpet snake's tongue licked at the air as the reptile came to a halt. It hissed, realising that something was not right with its environment. Spotting the hand that rested on the ground, the reptile struck out, its fangs sinking deep into the flesh. The corpse did not even flinch as the snake pumped venom into its stagnant veins. Instead, it saw the snake as something that was to be ingested. It wasn't sustenance that it craved, but the very life force itself: the reptile's spirit, its soul.

Pinning the creature to the ground, its fingers became claws, tearing at the snake's skin. Placing the lifeless carcass to its lips, it watched with curiosity as a white, vaporous substance escaped the cadaver. It began to gnaw at the raw flesh, slowly climbing to its feet.

Looking around, it saw the jeep to its right, a vague memory nagging at it. Contained within the object were two bright auras. Moving with purpose, it began to approach. The auras were strong, a vibrant blue that beckoned with promise. Neither aura stirred until…

Harper and Finney woke with a start. At first they thought they were dreaming: the vehicle was violently rocking on its own suspension. Their waking minds barely had chance to define the difference between reality and fantasy when a hand smashed through the window, grabbing Finney by the hair, trying to drag him out. His hands feebly scrabbled for a purchase on anything that would restrain his momentum.

As Finney's head was wrenched out of the window, he deciphered a black silhouette against the gloom of the night. There was vicelike pressure applied to his head and he screamed, trying to free his arms, which had become wedged in the window frame as shards of glass sliced into his forearms. He struggled against the grip, his pain beginning to intensify, until he heard something snap. It was as if the surrounding darkness had swallowed him completely.

Harper froze, unable to see beyond the impenetrable wall of darkness that surrounded him. He huddled in his seat, trying to curl himself into a ball. He could not block out the stomach-churning sounds that drifted through the encircling night. Reaching for the door handle, his palm brushed across the butt of his gun; the weapon reassured him and he thrust open the door. The night was palpable, rushing at him with force. Harper dived out into the darkness, aware that drifting in the tangible bleakness was the stench of cold death.

It was blinded by the radiance of life. Its desire to consume that essence was overwhelming. It was a fundamental instinct that was at its most raw. It watched a life form move away and it followed. The man was lit up like a beacon as he fled into the darkness.

The further Harper ran, the denser the darkness became. He could feel the wide-open space around him, yet he felt alone and hemmed in. Bordering on hysteria, he ran head-on into something that smelt rotten. Looking up, he stared at the man he had buried in the desert. A scream escaped his lips; it sounded hollow, like he was in some vast chamber. It was short-lived as the dead man struck him across the windpipe. Harper staggered forward, choking as the darkness descended on him again.

Quickly it descended on its prey, watching as the ethereal essence drained from the body. Leaving the man on the floor, it looked around, sensing a difference, as if it was no longer alone.

The killing now seemed to serve a purpose, sedating its desire, but it was not long before the zombie began to crave more of what it needed. It felt an unrestrained pull, the darkness becoming its caressing guide.

Colonel Windburn sat deep in contemplation; before him lay an ordnance map of Niger, in particular, a detailed satellite view of the Air Mountains. It was not one of the most hospitable environments on the planet. He had just returned from an in-depth meeting with the Ministry of Defence, where he'd had to explain the reality of the dire situation that now faced them.

His concentration was disturbed when a knock came on the door. 'Enter!' the Colonel barked gruffly. The door opened and in walked a young woman in Wrens' uniform.

'I think you should see this, Colonel!' She handed him a paper. 'It was sent to us via the service.'

The Colonel perused the content and noted from whom the communiqué had been sent. Cameron Ferguson was asking for orders.

'Did anything else come with it?' the Colonel asked.

'MI6 want to know what to do next, Whitehall is screaming for answers, and, in light of Sergeant Hornsby's report, intelligence are sitting on this until you issue your instructions.'

Windburn's face crinkled as he concentrated, looking at the communiqué. 'For the moment I want them to do nothing! There has been no confirmation that Ferguson is a renegade, but it would be prudent not to let him get wind that we are suspicious. Tell the service that everything is okay at this end and they are to inform Ferguson that he is to proceed as instructed.'

The shrill ringing of the telephone startled him from his deep concentration. He paused before answering. 'Windburn here!' Listening carefully he replied, 'Yes, sir!' and replaced the receiver on the cradle.

His brief conversation had gone some way to relieving his mind, but it had also posed a completely new set of problems to overcome. The telephone call had been from the Defence Minister, who had just come out of delicate negotiations with the

President of Niger. The President had given the go ahead for some sort of action to be taken against these international terrorists. He had also stipulated that his country was to lead the operation and the UN were to remain on an advisory basis. No move was to be made without his prior approval.

The problem was that the President had sanctioned the UN's involvement and not NATO's. In truth, this had created complications. Colonel Windburn didn't want the involvement of other countries in this. It was a British man in there, and the Colonel didn't necessarily want a United Nations operation. The operation was a specialist one, and the Colonel concluded that the best way forward would be to involve the Special Forces of the UN, which in turn meant that the British SAS and Captain Harrington's men would be involved in a big way.

The plan he had formulated in his mind should meet all of the necessary requirements. The move would meet with the President's strict stipulation of UN involvement, whilst the regiment would have the flexible power to do the job that was required.

Tracking its prey was no difficult thing: it could remain well out of sight yet know exactly where they were. Their psychic auras acted like a magnet, rushing to fill the void that was contained within it.

In the distance, a vehicle approached. Cocking its head to one side, its dead eyes were cast down.

The headlights of the oncoming vehicle grew in the darkness, coming together at the point where the zombie stood. The sudden illumination startling a scorpion that had come to a standstill on the toe of its boot. The vehicle came to a grinding halt, the headlights converging on a lone figure standing on the sand.

Slowly it raised its head, the ferociousness of the halogen beams reflecting from its dead eyes, giving them an iridescent glow. It appeared as a feral animal trapped within the beams of the headlights. It remained unmoving, its face lacklustre. Loud reports sounded in the stillness of the desert night. Sand spiralled into the air and six bullets repeatedly struck the upper torso of the inert zombie.

It felt none of the assault, but memories played at the forefront of its withering mind. The situation was familiar, one which it had been trained for in a former existence.

A Kalashnikov rifle hung from a strap from the zombie's shoulder, taken from its last kill. Bringing the weapon to bear, it pulled the trigger. The vehicle's headlights were immediately extinguished as bullets spat from the muzzle of the weapon.

Silently and furtively, it moved forward, homing in on its quarry. It stood on open ground mere feet from its aggressors, the extinguished light creating panic: they didn't know where it was. Crouching low, the corpse began to move forward with intent.

Ahead all was silent, the silence containing a portent of fear. These new impressions served to excite it, and it soundlessly homed in on its prey. There were two shots of blind panic as the Jack-thing reached the first of its victims; reaching out through the darkness, it seized the man. Its teeth bit into soft tissue, tearing off chunks of raw flesh. The scream was short-lived and died into the stillness of the night.

It was eager to take of the life force and brought its lips down hard onto the man.

An unshaven man wearing combats reached into the interior of the jeep for his weapon. He had a butt of a cigar clenched between his teeth and wore a cap back to front. His eyes were beady, unwavering. Looking across at his companion, he saw the sand rise up and swallow him whole.

He watched with excessive curiosity as the sand moved again. As he focused, he couldn't believe his eyes, realising his mistake too late. A figure loomed before him, hands pulling him down into oblivion.

The zombie finished dragging the second of its victims back to the jeep. It climbed into the driving seat, gunning the engine. It heard the summoning chant that was carried on the wind, a susurration that drifted through the darkness, leading it...

The entrance was well hidden. Even to the keenest eye, the rock face would not have given up its secret. But Samdi knew it was there, and so did the zombie.

It transferred the bodies of its victims from the back of the vehicle, placing them in their respective positions at the front. Contriving that the jeep continued on its course towards a sand dune not far from the mountain face, it lay on the ground, becoming one with the darkness.

The jeep hit the dune, its wheels spinning, digging it deeper and deeper into the loose sand.

The sun began to emerge in the east and movement from the mountain attracted its attention; the brilliant hue of life force emerged before it. Two men approached the vehicle.

Fragmented memories returned to it, about the life it had once led. It had been a soldier of some description.

Felix Grouper's eyes constantly flicked from one monitor to the next. Each screen revealed a view of outside the mountain. Three patrols had been sent out: none had returned. He was decidedly anxious.

Grouper had always been careful, concealing his tracks to a point where he became almost invisible. When he met Phillip Égalité, he found a man that understood his taste for the bizarre. Both men were from opposite ends of the scale, one wealthy, the other from the slums, who had to live like a reject within the boundaries of society.

Phillip Égalité had taken this reject, this pariah of vices, and moulded him into a creation of his own perverse design. Grouper became Égalité's disciple, whose wickedness and raw depravity were nurtured to the point of becoming art. He was Égalité's finest creation. And now Grouper's sanctuary was in danger of collapse.

Égalité had become sloppy, and Grouper was disgraced at being so easily taken in by this Jack Hornsby's charade. Grouper knew in the very pit of his stomach that something was out there. Either Jack Hornsby was still alive, or they had been sent by Jack.

Jack had become his nemesis, daring to tread where no other had. He had entered Grouper's inner domain, and Grouper was angered at how Égalité had denied him his chance of describing to Jack exactly how he had defiled his woman. As Grouper mused, he remembered the details of those hours leading up to the execution, when he had broken Lisa's resolve like that of a wild horse.

The door to the small office opened, and a swarthy-looking man entered the room. 'There is still no communication with unit four, sir!'

'And the other men that are missing?'

'Still no word!'

Grouper looked the man straight in the eye. 'I'd better take a look myself! You're with me!'

Grouper stood on the back of the vehicle, his hands clenched around a large-calibre machine gun, scanning the horizon for the slightest signs of movement.

In the distance, an object could be seen protruding from the sand. The object wavered in the intense heat. Grouper pulled a bandanna over the lower part of his face. As the vehicle turned, he felt the full force of the wind in his face. Determining that the object was a vehicle, he saw it sat at an odd angle, the front end dug into a sand dune. There was no movement from within, but the occupants were in plain view, slumped forward in their seats.

Grouper knew they were dead and he smiled. More than ever he now believed Jack to be alive. There was no one else; there had been no time for backup to be sent. Jack was provoking him, the challenge of a warrior from whom you could not turn away! When his vehicle stopped, Grouper jumped off the out board, investigating the vehicle.

His eyes beheld the carnage the vehicle contained. The first corpse was positioned in the driving seat, chest ripped apart; the second had been disembowelled, his entrails discarded about the jeep's interior. The smell was pungent, as flies buzzed eagerly about the jeep. Grouper breathed in the smell of death.

The wind had increased to an extent that the sand was being blown into an impenetrable wall around him. Striding back to his waiting vehicle, Grouper found himself fighting the gale. Invisible limbs grabbed at his every movement, attempting to sweep him off his feet.

Something here was wrong: he could feel it in his very being. Confirming his misgivings, voices rode the back of the sand-storm, screaming at him.

Grouper felt strange, cold with oscillating pinpricks that ran through his whole body. 'Dead!' the wind hissed at him.

'Come out!' Grouper screamed, his voice lost in the howling sandstorm. He was glad to return to the vehicle. 'Back to base!' he shouted, his mind disordered. He had seen Égalité shoot Jack! He had stood over the corpse. Yet he could not dispel the notion that the man was alive and well. 'If you want to play games, Jack, then let's play!'

Chapter 16

Égalité did not take the news lightly that Jack Hornsby, alias Jacob Portello, was still alive. His usual calm demeanour was transformed into that of a raging lunatic. As Kerry watched, she was horrified by what she perceived as a shadow drift across Égalité's eyes. His face appeared taut, the skin pulled tight around his skull, and something appeared to be undulating beneath his skin. His eyes had sunken into their sockets, and it was a stark transformation from a few hours earlier. Kerry thought his eyes were not human at all. Shuddering, she was repulsed.

Ferguson dared to interrupt Égalité. 'Nobody could have survived a point blank bullet to the heart!' This comment brought Égalité's ranting to a halt. He locked Ferguson in a deadly stare. 'There have been instances where the heart has kept beating, but he is dying even if he doesn't know it yet. The blood loss alone will finish him!'

Grouper sat regarding the table. When Ferguson had finished, he slowly raised his head. 'I'm not so sure!'

Ferguson gave a derisive laugh. 'There's only so much medical treatment a man can administer in the field. If, by some miracle, Jack is alive, then he will be weak: too weak to go around ripping people apart!'

'There was nothing weak about what was done to those men last night,' replied Grouper.

Ferguson smiled. 'Have it your own way, but I'm telling you that he's a dead man!'

O'Reilly listened to the exchange of words; he was a devout man, attending mass regularly. He had been there at Jack's execution, and he, if nobody else, was convinced that he was dead.

'Is it not conceivable,' he said, 'that Jack actually did get some kind of message through after all – or perhaps it was Duffy for that matter?'

Ferguson turned his attention to his Irish counterpart. 'Impossible!'

'Not so impossible. He was SAS, and I've seen how those bastards work. First they unnerve you, get you all spooked; then they rip you apart right down the middle!' O'Reilly made a line with his finger that led from his navel to his neck. 'It's an age-old strategy: divide and conquer!'

Grouper sat up in his chair paying more attention. 'So what you're saying is that there could be another out there?'

'As many as four! If you count Jack as one and Duffy as another, then there would be two more. Sabre teams, they call 'em. Always work in groups of four.'

Égalité, visibly calm now, appeared to be human again. 'Then we might be dealing with two men?' he asked.

'Well, it's more probable than dead men walking around exacting revenge, and I haven't heard of anybody returning from the grave since Jesus Christ himself!' Ferguson said, his dry humour falling flat as he was shot a warning glance from Égalité. The look was enough to turn his blood cold.

Kerry nervously twiddled her thumbs; she occasionally glanced up towards whoever was speaking. She had become subdued, wishing to God that none of this was really happening. She had to get out; things were going bad, and she foresaw them getting worse. Quickly rising from her seat, she spotted furtive movement from the corner of her eye. Concealed in the shadows at the end of the room she saw Samdi watching them, a smile adorning his face. How long he had been there Kerry had no idea; in fact, she was sure he hadn't been there before. An icy chill ran through her. Watching the shadows, she saw something unnatural about them, like they were contriving to conceal his presence.

O'Reilly rose from his seat, shaking his head. 'Shall we leave?' he asked. Kerry, who was eager to escape the confines of the room, rose to her feet. The atmosphere had become overbearing.

As they left, an untoward feeling compelled her to turn around; Samdi was gone, but the darkness remained where he had been. Leaving the room, she was startled by the manservant suddenly appearing before her. Kerry quickly skirted him.

Looking at O'Reilly, she muttered, 'I'm frightened!' O'Reilly placed a comforting arm around her shoulder.

'Things will be OK,' he stated in a voice that belied the conviction of his words. 'You and I are outta here!' O'Reilly sensed they were being followed and turned to see Grouper behind them.

He stood smiling. 'Deserting a sinking ship?' The accusation was direct and to the point. 'So you want out?' O'Reilly detected Grouper was playing with him.

'Did I say I was going anywhere?' O'Reilly said.

A cruel, lopsided grin manifested on Grouper's face. 'I couldn't help but overhear your conversation with Miss O'Moore, and forgive me if I received the wrong impression, but it sounded like desertion. I don't know what the IRA does with deserters, but where I come from they are shot!'

O'Reilly's eyes hardened with mock bravado. 'Is that a threat?'

Grouper smiled, an uneasy atmosphere hanging heavily in the air. 'You should know that I never make threats, Mr O'Reilly!' Looking at Kerry, he said, 'And fear not, Miss O'Moore; if Jack has been allowed a second chance by whatever God he worships, then rest assured that chance is all he's going to get!'

Chapter 17

The Apache helicopter swept across the barren desert landscape. The attack craft was fully laden with Hellfire laser-designated missiles, Hydra 70 folding-fin aerial rockets and a 30 mm M230 chain gun. With this much firepower, Grouper had the capacity to vaporise any living creature he found crawling upon the scorched sand. Scanning the desert floor, something shone in the distance.

'Put her down here!' he commanded, his voice rising above the noise of the rotors.

As the craft hovered, feet above the surface, Grouper opened the door and jumped out of the craft. Landing on the soft sand, he watched as the helicopter headed back to the mountains.

Alone, Grouper felt an uneasy stillness settle around him. Nothing but sterile, desiccated wasteland confronted him. The sands rippled, rising like graves of the forgotten gods. Grouper was left with an uncanny sensation – it felt as though something was watching him. Beginning to move, a desert wind ruffled his clothes. Alert, his senses became sharpened.

He felt a breath on the back of his neck. Spinning round, he discovered nothing was there. Turning back, he was challenged by Samdi's face engraved in a sand dune, laughing at him. As the wind blew, the face dissipated into the sand.

Grouper was unnerved. Producing a walkie-talkie, he ordered the helicopter to return and pick him up.

The zombie moved closer to the mountain of iniquity; it could feel the pull of living occupants like iron filings to a magnet. It stood, observing a large cave at the base of the mountains. Guards had been placed at the front and fragmented images came to it: five faces that were somehow connected. The thing began to advance.

As the zombie moved, it resembled a creature dragged from the abyss. Its features were of death, and it carried all men's worst fears of hell behind it.

Swinging its arm, the zombie struck an effective and deadly blow across the windpipe of one of the sentries. The man crumpled before the animated corpse. Shock and fear froze the second sentry, his weapon loosely aimed at the monstrosity, but his mind could not define the reality of what it saw.

The man's eyes met with those of the dead. Congealed blood smothered its mouth. His finger tightened on the trigger of his weapon as the zombie grabbed the barrel of the gun, twisting the weapon with ease. Forcing the barrel of the gun under the sentry's chin, the soldier found himself locked in a morbid staring contest with a dead and rotting corpse, repulsed by the foul odour of rotting flesh. To escape this horror the sentry pulled the trigger, preferring death to the torment he was forced to endure. The zombie retrieved his discarded weapon from the floor.

The zombie began to piece together fragmented images that flashed through its mind. Looking at its hands, it raised the weapon.

There was movement from inside the cave as multiple shots rang out. Bullets thudded into its torso, creating a macabre dance that knocked it down. The shots kept coming as the zombie again climbed to its feet.

Soldiers had taken refuge behind a vehicle, and the zombie turned, squarely facing them. Firing a bullet, the hot lead hit one of the men in the forehead as the remaining two began to slowly retreat. A stray bullet punctured the petrol tank. Fuel began to flood the floor as the zombie returned fire. There was a sudden whoosh and the cavern was engulfed in flame. An explosion followed, engulfing two of the soldiers.

Running, beating at their flaming bodies, they collapsed in a fiery heap on the floor, becoming one with the surrounding inferno. The door of an elevator slid effortlessly open, and the cadaver of Jack walked in.

Chapter 18

The zombie became one with the shadows, dissolving into blackness. A man passed by, and it recognised his face as one of those its decaying mind had seen before. It watched through a milky film, its eyes belonging to a world of maggots and worms. The name 'Grouper' drifted on a forgotten breeze, and it felt a vehement hatred. Grouper paused, turning briefly before quickly continuing on his way. The zombie was now firmly in the control of another, and Samdi would bend Jack's remains to his will.

Kerry sat on the bed in her allocated quarters. She had objected to being brought to the Air Mountain stronghold, but had been forced by a persuasive Grouper. There was nothing homely about her room; it was simple to the extreme. Consisting of a bed and toilet facilities, it reminded her of a prison cell. Her mind was locked within her own reverie. 'Jack's dead!' she repeated to herself. The solitary sound of her own voice, along with the memory, brought a single tear to her eye.

Why did the death of this one man leave her feeling empty? The time they had spent together had been brief. Kerry was a double agent, working for the opposite side, and Jack had been the enemy. She doubted her emotions. Things were becoming weird. She thought of Samdi standing in the shadows, of the way Égalité's facial features appeared to undulate. The mere thought of it sent shivers through her. Everybody appeared to be on edge. It was as if something dark and foreboding was gradually inching its way to the surface.

O'Reilly appeared to be outwardly the same, but his usual rough and unapproachable personality was subdued. The hideous Grouper was a nightmare!

Her thoughts returned to Jack, for whatever he had been, he had become a light amidst the surrounding darkness; she had felt safe under his watchful eye.

Sitting in the confines of this room, her mind alternated between the realities of the past and the present. She knew she'd been a fool to fall in love; she had made herself a casualty of her own heart. Now she was afraid that this time she had been drawn into a situation she was unable to walk away from.

The frustration of sitting had made time immobile. Irritated, she flicked a lock of hair away from her eyes; she was deep in thought, listening to the silence that surrounded her. This isolation unnerved her.

The zombie entered a room that was reminiscent of a radio repair shop. Wires hung from racks; computer chips, transistors and diodes were housed in a small cabinet that hung on the wall. An oscilloscope and soldering iron were positioned on a small workbench that was littered with circuit boards. The zombie appeared to survey the room. Someone was approaching. The area became cast in deep, impenetrable shadow.

Cameron Ferguson pushed O'Reilly into the room. 'The man is paranoid! And so are you. There is absolutely no way that HQ suspects me. I've covered my tracks too well!'

'I hope you're right,' O'Reilly sneered, his rough Irish brogue conveying his personal misgivings. Looking up at Ferguson, he continued. 'If Jack did leave word, then they will be down on us like a ton of bricks!'

Ferguson laughed. 'You're as bad as the rest of them, jumping at shadows! It seems that they don't make the Irish freedom fighter like they used to!'

His sarcastic barb pierced O'Reilly, and his eyes narrowed.

Smiling through gritted teeth, he hissed. 'If we were in Ireland you would be a dead man! Mark my words, no one insults Shamus O'Reilly! So when you're away from here, and if ye happen to be in the green country, I'd watch my back, because you're a dead man!'

Ferguson grinned, paying no real heed to the Irishman's threat. 'Why! What happened to the famous Irish humour?'

With no further discussion, O'Reilly stormed out of the room.

Left on his own, Ferguson turned, chuckling to himself. He had intended to bait the Irishman, and he had succeeded. Then he noticed movement within the darkness. He strained his eyes, trying to penetrate the obscurity. Again there was movement, a shadow gliding within a shadow. He was about to shout a challenge when the room became subdued by a heavy omnipresence; the air was thick and robbed him of breath. Ferguson distinctly heard movement, and the room smelt like something had died.

Reaching for his gun, his hand reassuringly grasped the butt of the weapon. Hefting it before him, he thumbed the safety into the off position. 'Who's there?' he challenged, putting command and authority into his voice. Silence was the only reply he received. Long moments passed before a screeching startled him.

The rational world had suddenly become a delirium of twisted nightmares. The screeching changed tempo, into that of frenetic laughter. He scrutinised the shadows. The entire room was alive with twisting shapes of a diabolic magnitude. Fear taking control, he fired, as a hand knocked the gun from his grasp. He heard it clatter on the floor, and was left staring at a worn and rotting hand. Grasped by his lapels, he was lifted off his feet and found himself face to face with the drawn and lifeless visage of Jack Hornsby. He felt his bowels liquefy.

Struggling in the zombie's grasp, Ferguson fought to break free. He rained ineffectual blows upon the corpse, then felt himself thrust away, landing heavily on the floor. He was winded and frantically scrabbled for his gun. Ferguson dared to glance upward. There the zombie stood, a grotesque testament to its former glory. The face was hideously disfigured. Out of the corner of his eye, Ferguson glimpsed the gun. His eyes locked with that of the dead Jack Hornsby. 'What do you want?' he screamed at the cadaver. His only chance of survival now depended upon making a lunge for the weapon.

The zombie reached down as Ferguson scrambled toward the gun. He felt his feet grasped and was dragged backwards away from his goal. Lying on his back, the entire weight of the living corpse pressed down upon him. Clenching his fist, he punched at the face of his dead attacker with no effect. Straightening his fingers, Ferguson came up under the ribcage as he had been taught in training.

Beginning to scream, his cries were cut off by the zombie's hand. A decayed palm spread across his mouth, the fingers spaced across the bridge of his nose. The pressure was intense, and Ferguson began to convulse.

The zombie turned away from the form of Ferguson, a deep and bellowing laugh echoing inside the room.

The screaming brought O'Reilly to a standstill. Turning back, he thought it sounded like Ferguson. O'Reilly knew that Ferguson was a wild card – he had never liked or trusted the British. He retraced his steps slowly. There were sounds of a scuffle coming from within the room.

He reached forward, grasping the door handle. The door swung inward, and O'Reilly saw the sprawled, lifeless body of Ferguson, He hesitated, but a morbid curiosity took hold of him. Stepping forward, he saw another figure in the room. Slowly, the aggressor turned round to face him. O'Reilly was shocked and mortified at the sight he beheld. The door slammed shut behind him. 'Mother of God!' he said, making the sign of the cross.

O'Reilly spun on his heels, thrusting the door wide and slamming it firmly behind him. He watched with frantic hysteria as the door began to open again. Fingers that were blotched and decayed pushed their way out, grasping a hold of the door. He tried barricading the door with the weight of his body, when a gunshot sounded, and O'Reilly was violently flung away from the door.

In the face of his terror, he managed a smile. 'Well, Jack, me lad. It seems the last laugh is yours!' He received a bullet dead centre of his forehead.

Chapter 19

Two squadrons of the SAS had been flown into Niger and were awaiting orders. When those orders had arrived, immediate action was taken and the ground-level entrance to Phillip Égalité's invisible complex was under close observation. The Government of Niger had recognised the seriousness of the problem and had given its cooperation to the United Nations, who were there strictly on an advisory basis. The plan that had been formulated was for Captain Harrington and his squadron to create enough confusion for the Fist of Euskadi to reveal their presence. Using the Niger air force, the plateau Jack had described would be bombarded from the air. From what Jack had said in his report, the nuclear missiles were being kept deep within the mountain. Niger's army would then engage the enemy, allowing the SAS to gain entry to the complex. From Jack's report, they had understood that the nuclear weapons were being stored below sea level, and the plan was to drain the oasis, flooding the lower part of the complex. The controlled blast would cause a nuclear reaction where a majority of the radiation would be absorbed by the water. The SAS would move in from both upper and ground entrances into the mountain. The only flaw in the plan was that an explosion within the heart of an extinct volcano might awaken Mother Nature's fury.

Peering out across the desert landscape, Grouper scanned for any signs of movement; he spotted two advance teams heading towards the mountain. He identified the advance task force, knowing that behind them would be a main strike force consisting of an armoured division! Grouper knew that they couldn't make a fight of it.

He now wished that he had listened to his gut feelings. Now a force of trained and disciplined men was heading towards them, and ultimately Grouper knew that it was going to be a bloodbath!

Concealed less than a mile away, Captain Graham Harrington watched from ground level. He and his Sabre squadron of fifteen men had already located the mountain entrance and placed plastic high explosives, which could be detonated via satellite. They had witnessed the aftermath of some kind of battle. He was now waiting for the aerial assault, which would signal the beginning of the operation.

Harrington looked skyward when he heard the first of the jets; a sonic boom resonated in the air.

In total, thirty-two troopers lay hidden on the desert floor. Another thirty-two men were climbing the mountain from the opposite side. If all was going to plan, they were already in place, allegedly operating within the boundaries of the UN command, and were forbidden to engage in any gunplay unless fired upon themselves. In a mission such as this, every person involved knew that this was just political jargon used to cover the British government against any international outcry. There was no way in which they could lead an assault and not come under fire, but the ruling was there, and to a certain extent they had to abide by it.

As the first of the aerial missiles was released, the aircraft came in low. A loud explosion resonated through the mountains. The mountains themselves were immense eruptions of black, volcanic rock, created from the planet's core. Although the volcanoes were extinct and had been for millennia, there was still a probability that seismic activity could trigger a chain reaction below the earth's surface. It was a risk, but not a bigger risk than the mission itself. If successful, they would seal the uranium and the Fist of Euskadi in the earth for ever. In synchronisation with the missile's explosion, Harrington sent a signal to the overhead satellite, detonating the explosives at the ground entrance.

Sirens blared as doors were sealed. The entire facility was on alert; Grouper had ensured that both of the entrances were covered by a contingent of men. Soon it would be every man for himself.

Hurriedly, he made his way to the base of the complex. The earlier explosion had done little structural damage, and in light of this new onslaught Grouper thought that he might have been hasty in assuming that Jack was still alive. Things were turning sour fast, and although Grouper was standing true to his obligations, the time to bail was drawing ever closer.

Three men raced towards the scene of the explosion. Grouper ordered them to stop and follow him. Descending a final flight of stairs, the four men were greeted by billowing smoke. His military mind made a calculated assumption. With an air strike it made sense that a frontal attack force would remain out of the line of fire until the bombardment was over. With the complex being situated within the heart of a volcanic mountain, the attack would be minimal, designed to knock out any response force that they might have, also providing a tactical diversion for a ground force to make a move.

The smoke cleared, and Grouper's countenance was grim. 'They're coming!' he said.

The puppet master now had new designs for his animated corpse. Simultaneous explosions distracted Samdi's attention. Things were beginning to occur that he had not foreseen. Seeing all, through the lifeless eyes of Jack, Samdi prowled the complex, silently moving through the network of corridors.

The first explosion rocked the entrance; the entire chamber was bathed in fire. The scene was followed up with repeated gunfire. Viewing all from his link with the corpse, Samdi saw Grouper's large form rise up from the smoke, entering the affray. He held a light automatic weapon at his hip which spat deadly loads into the confusion ahead.

All is well, Samdi thought. Grouper was still alive, and it was upon Grouper that Samdi desired revenge most of all. Bit by bit, piece by piece, each of Samdi's visions had materialised. Grouper was nothing but a tyrant with twisted perversions. If he knew how he was being used as a pawn on an astral chessboard, Samdi knew he would be dead, but that was all part of his revenge. The time would come when all would be revealed.

Samdi maintained the corpse in its position, concealing it with shadow, observing as a force of troopers stormed the entrance. The air was alive with gunfire, the attack force beginning to make headway. Grouper's men fell like flies.

Grouper knew that now was the time to bail. Desertion was something that came naturally to him: self-preservation was always at the forefront of his mind. A man broke cover from the front, rushing towards him. His weapon must have jammed because he screamed his defiance at Grouper, not decreasing his momentum. Grouper rose to the challenge.

He thrust his arm out, catching the man's neck, snapping his elbow up and twisting at the same time, dislocating it. Taking a quick survey of the situation, Grouper saw that a majority of his men were dead. There were still small pockets of resistance, but he judged that they could not hold out much longer.

Moving backwards, he made for the stairwell. The lift had been put out of commission, the doors blown inward from the blast. The stairwell reeked of rotting meat and Grouper felt an icy shard enter his being. All he could think about was staying alive as he sensed something reaching up and out of the darkness; he urged himself on that much faster.

Taking check, Grouper took the next door out of the stairwell and found himself in a deserted corridor. It didn't take him long to recognise where he was. He heard a strange chant that echoed around him. Compelled to investigate, he moved towards the source of the sound with care, looking in every room as he went. At the end, he saw an open door. Proceeding with caution, Grouper reached for his weapon, but his hand grasped at nothing.

Samdi sat cross-legged in the middle of the floor; behind him was an altar, the remains of a dead animal upon the surface. He sat in a circle of black candles. Standing before each candle were crude effigies of native African origin. Samdi's eyes were closed, the unnerving chant issuing from his lips.

Grouper became enraged, knowing that the servant was somehow responsible. Taking a step towards him, Grouper was seized in an invisible grip. He could not move: he was paralysed, a human statue observing Samdi through fearful eyes. A figure that reeked of death moved slowly past him. As he watched in horror, the form turned, revealing itself to be the ravaged remains of Jack Hornsby.

Unable to tear his gaze away, Grouper watched as Samdi opened his eyes, laughing. Looking at the zombie, he watched it open its mouth and a smoky mist gushed forth. The vapours eddied and swirled around it, forming a billowing cloud that moved with purpose as it spread around the room. Grouper wanted to run, but found himself trapped in a fog that came up to his knees. Suddenly he was released from the indiscernible grasp, feeling true fear for the very first time in his life.

'Run!' Samdi said, still laughing. 'Run while you can!'

Grouper watched the fog consume the Bokor, dissolving him into nothing. Then he was gone. Breaking into a run, Grouper stumbled out of the room, the ground fog lapping at his heals. Fearing for his life, he ran.

The zombie followed as Grouper found himself confronted by a wall of fog. Disorientated, he stumbled into one of the rooms.

He knew that he could not stay where he was. Trying to regulate his breathing, he listened for movement in the hallway. Hearing none, he slowly opened the door, only to be confronted by Jack's motionless cadaver. Faced with a moment of indecision, Grouper froze.

A macabre stand-off ensued. Taking a step forward, he tested the way, the zombie remained inactive, waiting for hidden instructions. Breaking into a run, Grouper headed for the stairwell. The fog wasn't as thick here and Grouper saw his lost weapon lying on the floor. Leaping for it, he shoulder-rolled, coming up with the gun in his hand and fired twice in succession. Both of the high-velocity, hollow-tipped rounds hit the zombie squarely in the chest, ripping away sinew and rotting tissue. He pulled the trigger again and the hammer fell on an empty chamber. Throwing the useless weapon at the corpse, Grouper shouted his defiance.

'What the fuck are you?'

The zombie faltered in its advance, cocking its head to one side. A dead silence invaded the hallway. Then a sinuous whisper fluttered in the fetid air, the words merely perceived opposed to being heard. 'Surely you did not think I was going to let you off that easily did you?' Grouper knew it was the voice of Samdi.

Darting into another room, he ran straight towards a mahogany desk. The room he was in was Égalité's. He knew that he kept a Colt automatic in a secret compartment. Locating the clasp, the gun slipped effortlessly into his hand. Placing the weapon down, he felt about inside until he had located two spare magazines.

A shadow drifted across him as the undulating whisper resounded again. 'Are you scared, Felix?'

Shouting in sheer defiance, Grouper answered, 'You're dead, and it's about time you realised that! Dead! Dead and buried!'

A devilish cackle filled Felix's head. 'Oh he's dead… But not buried!'

Grouper's eyes continually scanned the room, his surroundings beginning to press in upon him. In a high and trembling voice, he shouted out, 'Why don't you come out and face me like a man?' He began to laugh. 'What's the matter? Don't you like heaven?' His hysterical cackle echoed again.

The silence was tangible as Grouper heard the rustle of movement behind him. He swung round, the gun held steadfast in his hand, when his arm was seized, and he was propelled forward, crashing into the wall. The gun fell from his grasp.

Jarred and shaken, Grouper went after the weapon. He felt hands seize his shoulders, and he was lifted effortlessly to his feet. He looked with consternation-filled eyes, imagining that he saw a smirk touch the slack, dead lips of Jack.

The zombie now had Grouper's throat in its rotting hand. It began to squeeze until the fingers broke into the flesh. Making a tight fist, the zombie tore the tissue away.

Gagging, Grouper's hands instinctively flailed at his throat. His eyes wide with terror and disbelief, he fell to the ground, staring at his harbinger of death.

Chapter 20

Captain Harrington and his squadron searched the lower levels of the complex. Laying charges as they went, they had still not located the missiles. The explosions would ensure that the lower levels would be submerged under water.

It was imperative they locate the missiles or the whole mission would be compromised. Exploring the tunnels, the symbol for radiation was prominently displayed on a closed door before him. Harrington was confident that this was where the missiles were being kept. On opening the door, he hit the payload. There the missile carriers stood brooding, rockets of annihilation sleeping on their backs. It took Harrington minutes to discover that they had been booby-trapped.

The explosive device was active, connected to a mercury switch; there was no timer. Knowing time was of the essence, Harrington was fast running out of options. 'We can't risk moving it, we can't disarm it.'

'Boss, maybe we can slow it down. Give us all chance to get clear before the charges go off?' Simon Smith, a long-standing member of the SAS, spoke words of wisdom, but his voice was unconvincing.

'Have we got time before this whole place comes down on our heads?' Harrington asked.

The loud report of echoing gunshots alerted the men. There was a brief pause, and then the screaming began. Harrington moved to the door, looking out along the corridor. What he saw made him scrabble to place a black gas mask over his face.

'Gas!' he screamed. Harrington beheld a smoky effluvium slowly creeping along the floor. It was roughly knee-high and moved with the swell of an incoming tide. The sound of screaming was cut dead, leaving a deathly silence in its wake. Harrington watched the creeping fog, realising there was something peculiar about it. It moved with a purpose that left the impression it was alive.

Slowly and intentionally, it lapped Harrington's feet, creeping further into the chamber. Even beneath their masks, they detected a strange odour that oozed with a prevailing sense of evil.

The men backed off, feeling something about the fog spoke of death. As they retreated, the fog advanced towards them.

Harrington's concerns were aired on interlinked transmitters that all the men wore under their masks. 'Watch it lads! I don't know what this stuff is, but I suggest that we don't hang around to find out!'

Strange moaning sounds came from all around them. Harrington felt uneasy and was loath to move from the room but knew that if they didn't they would be at a tactical disadvantage. Having no other choice, they ventured out into the fog. It lapped at their legs, exploring them.

Sounds of low moaning filled the corridors, the noises not natural, leaving the men uneasy. Harrington believed that the sounds were human, and these thoughts of mortal adversaries went some way to reassuring him. If it was a human sound, then it could be killed! Moving steadily through the mist, they found the corridors deserted. A hollow wailing echoed around them, emanating from the fog itself.

Sensing the encroachment of danger, the four men stood back to back, covering every angle of their environment. The problem of the nuclear missiles temporarily forgotten, they readied their weapons. Shapes began to rise up out of the fog, and the source of the loathsome groaning became apparent.

There were dozens of them, all slowly ambling with twisted, loping gaits towards them. Harrington saw his own men, fresh blood glistening on their ravaged corpses. The spectacle served to bewilder, the fog clinging to the dead forms like wispy cloaks, swirling and eddying around them. It appeared to be growing, as if it were feeding upon its own existence.

Harrington's men were not the only victims of this bizarre reanimation: other corpses joined them.

Captain Harrington refused to believe what he saw; he was a soldier, a practical man, and the brutality of callous carcasses standing before him was an impossibility that he could not accept.

The men waited for the onslaught of the damned. Graham

Harrington was unable to dispel the notion that he was seeing things because of inhalation of the gas. Each man was frozen to the spot, watching the march of the dead.

The SAS team chose not to wait any longer. With a unified precision they opened fire as one, the loads from their weapons cutting the walking corpses down. But the respite was short-lived as each slain zombie rose to continue its advance. With the rear closed, the soldiers now had no other option but to continue deeper into the facility.

It was now a certainty that this was no hallucination, collectively or otherwise. It was real. The stairwell now represented their only means of escape, and moving in that direction they sent a final burst of gunfire into the cadaverous mob.

Harrington led his team out of the corridor and into a large storage area; the fog lay ankle deep. Each man was on edge, their fear confirmed by their silence. This was the unknown, where nightmares became reality. They had received no training that could have possibly prepared them for a situation such as this.

Harrington's first priority was the completion of his mission; the second was the safety of his men. Standing at the bottom of the stairway, the Captain's priorities were reordered. Getting out became the foremost priority, even if he could only tell the world what he had seen. Cautiously they began to ascend the staircase.

Harrington and his men were plunged into total chaos. The loss of light submerged them into irrevocable darkness, each man discarding his gas mask to adopt his night vision goggles. They had been engaged in a desperate struggle with a hoard of the undead when the lights had been extinguished and all was submerged into disordered darkness. The legion of death had been gaining ground when the lights went out, and now indeterminate seconds passed in total darkness, the only light available emitted from flaming weapons to guide their ineffective gunplay. Nothing prevented the demons from advancing. A cry of extreme agony went out into the darkness and, to his consternation, Harrington saw one of his men being dragged off by four of the things. He smashed the stock of his weapon into the face of an advancing demon.

The abomination went down as Harrington scurried out of its reach. The demon rose like a fallen angel of hell. Fast thinking was what was needed now! He saw that two of his men, Mills and Cutter, had regrouped at the end of the corridor and were standing by an erstwhile unnoticed exit.

The bloodthirsty zombies were for the time being intent upon their one victim, as they clamoured to get their pound of flesh. Dyer's screams of profound torment died away. Only the insidious ripping sounds of the zombies rupturing his remains could be heard echoing through the silence.

Harrington had no time for deliberation: he was aware of more pitiless movement behind him. Thrusting himself forward, he ran at full pelt, his rapid movement attracting the attention of the feasting zombies. Cutter saw his commander's plight and raised his weapon, sending a burst of fire into the host behind. His attack had little effect, as more of the voracious monstrosities joined the throng. *En masse*, the dead advanced, a repulsive accumulation of virulent deformities carrying favours of death.

A burst of fire came from the evil dead, and Cutter caught a bullet in the stomach. Harrington was loath to close the door after Mills had followed him, but Cutter defiantly remained on the outside, waving them on. No amount of cajoling could deter him from his self-appointed task. The ungodly mass was advancing, creeping steadily forward inch by inch.

One such cadaver, the decrepit remains of Felix Grouper, had advanced in such a manner. Low to the ground it had crept; what decaying memories it had possessed in life, the undead thing now used in death. Cutter stood a few feet before it, continuing to fire what the zombie vaguely remembered to be a gun. Reaching forward with a claw-like hand, it grasped the right calf of its victim, yanking him forward into the throng.

Harrington and Mills watched with mounting horror as Cutter was pitched forward into the ravenous hoard. His weapon remained firing for a few seconds after he was consumed by the mass, and stopped as he began to scream. Harrington could watch no longer, the nightmare gnawing at his sanity. Closing his eyes, he thought of the downed man, all the dignity of the once-warrior stripped from him in death.

Survival was now of the uttermost importance. Slamming the door shut, blocking out the horror, Captain Harrington held it closed while Mills tried to locate a means of securing it. There was a metal cabinet, which he stumbled across in the darkness, and now the two men dragged it into a position where it was propped at an angle, leaning on the door. Their task complete, the two men turned in the one direction left open to them and peered into the darkness. They were in a corridor. A conduit straight to hell, Harrington thought.

'Let's move!' he said, his quietly spoken words shattering the still silence.

Neither man spoke, each embodied with his own unspoken conceptions of their grotesque plight. Thirty-two men of the elite SAS had entered the facility under the direct command of Captain Graham Harrington. Each man was a highly trained and capable individual. Apart from the exchange of orders, each member of the squadron was isolated and alone with nothing but their thoughts to keep them company. Now only two remained! They had seen nothing of the other squadron that had formed the spearhead of the attack, their communications equipment was inoperable, and they were stumbling around in the dark with no idea of where they were.

The Nite-Lites designated that shallow illumination was being discharged from somewhere ahead of them. The meagre luminance offered a welcome return to their restricted vision. The two men advanced with both expeditiousness and discretion. There was presently no need to use the Nite-Lite goggles, as enough light was being emitted for them to see by. Both men checked that their weapons were loaded and moved in a swift and precise manner.

What challenged their eyes when they arrived at the opening overwhelmed them into a moment of indecision. The two SAS veterans were confronted by yet another horror. An undead demon had a grasp of a man's throat. They both viewed the scene with a somewhat detached impartiality. Both Harrington and Mills opened fire at the exact same moment, their hatred towards these heinous and ungodlike creatures spilling forth from the barrels of their weapons, each bullet a personal vendetta for a lost comrade. Two guns firing at will, their vengeance shattered the silence with intended death.

The explosion rocked the facility to its core; the fluctuations of the thermal convulsion rippled beneath their feet. It was the signal for Captain Harrington and Trooper Mills to leave with the utmost haste. Harrington knew his orders were specific. He and his squadron were to contain and minimise the effects of a nuclear explosion. The second SAS squadron, in accordance with their original orders, had laid and set a trail of high explosives throughout the upper levels of the facility.

Satellite and thermal imaging had showed the facility to be partly contained within a sill of the volcano. The main ground level entrance was close to the throat, and the second squadron had set a large concentration of explosives with the intention of blowing a hole directly through to the throat of the volcano and possibly precipitating a volcanic eruption. This was a double-edged sword because if both phases were successful, and after the sub levels had been submerged, then the volcanic eruption itself would absorb another percentage of the radiation. It was hoped that the lava flow would seal the entire area for the foreseeable future. It was a gamble, but the eyes of the world were now focused upon the success of this mission. The possibility that Niger could get their hands on a nuclear weapon was another consideration.

The construction of the facility had been very daring. As much as it had been virtually invisible, part of the structure, which followed natural conduits in the mountain, traversing the main chimney of the volcano itself. The Air Mountains had not seen a major volcanic eruption in millions of years.

Forthwith it emerged that the hand of God was being employed through the elite men of the British SAS, as a second explosion swayed the complex. Captain Harrington squandered no more time, and the two men rapidly disappeared in an attempt to locate a way out of this living mausoleum. They did not stay to see the zombie rise from the floor.

Chapter 21

Kerry couldn't shake the feeling that something was seriously wrong. It had slowly crept up on her, rudely enforced by an explosion that shook the rock beneath her. Her preoccupied thoughts were silenced as the ominous sound brought forward feelings of disquietude.

Listening intently, she heard nothing but silence, and mounting apprehension forced her to venture out, witnessing an outlandish-looking fog that moved in a tide along the corridor. Kerry believed there was a fire and stood for indecisive seconds.

The fog began to swell, slowly filling the corridor. Kerry was blinded as it closed in around her. It contained a strange smell that became almost addictive. She was disorientated, panic welling within her. She could make out blurred silhouettes that surfaced and fluxed before her. These spectres of gloom drifted with a slow and indolent tempo. Feeling isolated and forsaken, she became lost within the obscurity of her own fears.

She shouted out as something brushed against her arm, making her spring back. She was grabbed by something deathly cold. Turning, the most hideous sight greeted her. The man – for that was what it had once been – had no real face; the skin had been flayed from the skull, and one of its eyes hung by tenuous nerves from the socket. Its mouth was a hollow orifice that yawned in monstrous mockery. What skin remained was charred black, and she could smell the fetor of burnt flesh.

She screamed, lashing out at the thing, shoving it away. The transgressing hands removed, Kerry ran into the eddying fog. Finding herself back in her room, she slammed the door shut, making it an inescapable refuge from the marauding dead that roamed the open corridors beyond. Looking around her, Kerry piled what she could against the door. Effectively she had created a prison within a sepulchre of the living dead. Kerry collapsed to the floor, realising that in her damnation there was no prospect of release, no hope of escape.

Taking a bitter breath, dread subdued her limbs as she became aware of scuffling from the other side of the door. The sound was slow and assiduous. Holding her breath, she heard a second explosion from above; then something struck the door. Deep within her heart she had known that it would come to this; it was only a matter of time before the hoards of hell descended upon her for her selfish sins.

Kerry had always carried an awful lot of pride and vanity. These iniquities were her trophies of worth. They had forged a barrier that shielded the little girl who still dwelt deep down from a dark and cruel world.

Her eyes were wide, staring as the door handle began to slowly turn, the door opening slowly as if the nefarious miscreant savoured the fear inside. The door struck the barrier and bloodless fingers curled around the partially open door. Kerry watched, frozen with fear. The makeshift barricade offered little resistance as inch by inch the door made headway.

Fog flowed like a living carpet into the room, filling it. Kerry curled herself into a tight ball, a last defence against an inescapable outcome. Framed in the doorway was the decomposing cast of a former person. The zombie's head rose as it stepped into the room and looked in the general direction of Kerry.

Her throat was parched and she tried hard to swallow. Holding her eyes shut, she coveted isolation within the sombre vacuum of herself and was startled by a voice. It came from nowhere, yet it was everywhere. It could not have been uttered from any lips of the living. Its pestilent timbre sent shards of ice through her body.

Forcing her eyes open, she gazed upon her tormentor and was mortified to discover the corpse had decrepit resemblance to Jack Hornsby. That long-dead voice kept her in terrified rapture. 'Kerry, Kerry!'

'Go away!' she screamed, placing her hands to her head. 'Go away, go away! You're not real!' She looked upon the dead man.

Kerry's mind became an unqualified entanglement of reality and nightmare; the codes of rationality could not now be adhered to. In this ghastly situation, Kerry was bordering her wit's end.

Yet the proof stood before her, a loathsome violation of creation. She faltered, looking upon the vacuous husk of Jack. It was unmindful of her. Kerry quickly regained her composure. The zombie did not move.

Samdi sat cross-legged in his temple. The connection he had made with the zombie was both exhausting and rewarding at the same time. Now the ultimate revenge was his; all of his enemies lay at his feet. No longer the manservant, the joke, the Kaffir! Now Samdi was a power, a true power amongst mortals. And now he could take his rightful place among the gods of men.

He could see everything through the eyes of a now dead Jack. He found this amusing. Laughing loudly, his voice boomed in the silence. Watching Kerry cringe in fear, Samdi willed the corpse forward, placing thoughts of cold murder in its decaying mind.

Another explosion rocked the mountain and Samdi's trance-like state was threatened. He sensed a powerful presence in the room with him. Fatigue dogged him: he felt weary and threatened. Quickly relinquishing control of the dead Jack, Samdi became weak. He knew he could not succumb to weakness now. Too much depended on the outcome, and he was increasingly aware of the growing presence around him.

Opening his eyes, he saw nothing but the fog. A form materialised in the mist. At first he thought it to be one of the undead minions he had created. As it moved closer, realisation dawned on him. The form was none other than his dead son. 'Stop this now, Father. *Oludumare* and the *Orisha* forbid it.'

Samdi grinned. 'You are nothing more than a spirit, my son, a memory sent by the *Orisha* to torment me, to delay me from my task! Neither you nor the ancient gods have the power to stop me now.'

Samdi waved his hand dismissively and the boy dissipated, leaving Samdi alone. Closing his eyes, he connected with Jack's corpse, but this time he sensed he was not alone in the void's husk. This time something else was animating the corpse.

The zombie suddenly turned, ambling back the way it had come. Kerry felt alone, strangely deserted; contemplating her own survival, she thought back to when she had first met Jack.

Although she had flaunted all the poise of a tough Belfast girl, she had found herself internally swooning. This admirable and hardy stranger presented her affections with a complex combination of lust and extreme danger.

Now she felt a need to follow. For reasons unknown to her, she was no longer afraid; she felt calm. Jack was now a desecration upon existence itself! Amid her blindness, a continually assenting fragment of her soul began upon a journey of its own; this piece of her psyche began to question the reality of her actions. What did she hope to gain? Jack wasn't Jack, there was no person, just a mindless husk, an unsightly death relic.

Explosions echoed through the corridors behind her as she felt the very ground beneath her feet begin to tremble. Travelling along a damp, dark corridor, the fog petered out to ground level. Kerry could see light pinpointed ahead of her, yet the gloomy surroundings meant that she had lost sight of the dead Jack. She had been walking in an upward direction, and the light became her beacon of hope.

The whole mountain began to violently shake. Kerry was thrown to the floor and her heart pounded with increased vigour. She felt a hand clasp around her ankle. Images of the walking dead rushed her mind as debris began to fall from above. Kerry kicked out at the offending hand, overwhelmed with fear and a sudden feeling of claustrophobia. She wanted out of this pit! She became aware of a voice from behind her. It was a real voice that had no dead stigma attached to it.

Looking back, Kerry watched as a dirty and bedraggled face came up out of the darkness. A large gash was evident on his forehead. His eyes were almost pleading when he drew himself level with her. He wore combat fatigues that bore no insignia or rank. 'Christ!' he said. 'I thought everyone was dead!'

Kerry looked again at the opening ahead of them. 'They are!' she said, rising shakily to her feet, seeing the prone corpse of Jack lying face down, unmoving. As the two figures passed, the corpse began to stir. Moving with urgency, the two survivors became aware of the rumblings below as pressure continued to build.

They loomed onto the plateau like two bedraggled fiends emerging from the depths of Hades. The spectacle that confronted them was one of devastation, the dead were strewn about the ground, scattered in various poses of unspeakable death.

Graham Harrington surveyed the ruin. He paid particular attention to the sulphurous gas that was escaping from the fissures; it smelt of rotten eggs. It was not the foulness or the sickening vapour that engaged his regard. He appeared to seek something, his eyes alert and sharp as his attention was drawn to an Apache helicopter that appeared to be intact.

Guiding Kerry, he moved towards the helicopter. Kerry tried to avert her gaze, but her eyes were drawn to the lifeless corpses that littered the ground. They began to move, as a chorus of unearthly groans rose up into the air. This cadence of disconsolate discord sent violent spasms coursing through her. Her heart froze and she watched in total horror as the dead began to rise.

Panic-stricken, Kerry discovered that she was being dragged across the perilous and disordered terrain. As they arrived at the helicopter, the multitude of carcasses rose to their feet, moving steadily towards them. Graham struggled with the door to the cockpit, his haste disjointing his actions into a series of ineffective movements. Kerry risked a glance to where the unholy mass was advancing. At the head of the throng was a corpse that was all too familiar to her.

She was now aware of the extent to which Jack's corpse was ravaged and decayed, unlike the hoard that followed in his wake. His was not the most gruesome corpse that Kerry had encountered, but it was the most disturbing. He moved at a faster pace than the others of his sacrilegious brethren. The corpse was suddenly upon them as Graham gained entry to the helicopter. No sooner had he climbed aboard than Kerry was shoved into the craft, closely followed by the zombie.

The rotors began to turn, and a whine erupted from the turbines. Should the concourse of walking dead reach them, the chances of being able to take off were slim.

As the rotors built up speed, the first of the hideous parodies reached the chopper. It was a visage of total horror, its gullet ripped out, and it was conspicuous in its ragged array of exposed tissue and twisted sinew. Its face was pressed hard against the glass window as the chopper slowly began to rise. There was a tumultuous grumble, and a tremendous explosion ensued. The fury occurred with such ear-splitting violence that Graham, who was piloting the helicopter, was rendered temporarily deaf.

Multitudinous boulders of various shapes and sizes were tossed wildly into the air. These small asteroids shone with an orange luminance which threatened to rival the greatest star of all, the sun! Jagged, glowing rock rained down before the helicopter in a sight that created both awe and terror.

The rush of molten blaze surged up and out of the volcanic crevasses, the tide of consuming magma engulfing everything that stood upon the face of the plateau. Every orifice, every pothole was spilling forth liquid fire, which came with wanton abandonment.

The skill of the pilot meant the helicopter was able to avoid the engulfing death in his desperate bid to keep himself and the girl alive. Taking a deep breath of offensive air, he thanked his good fortune. Instantly, and with unbelievable speed, he withdrew his side arm, and turned back to confront the monster. His arm was met with a vice-like grip. He became rigid at the hold; the purchase was like that of hard ice, and it felt as though he had plunged his arm into a vat of nitrogen. His fatigues offered no defence against this kind of frigidity as his eyes beheld the remains of Jack. Graham felt fear take his soul as a scream of sheer terror welled deep within him.

The zombie retrieved the weapon from Graham's grasp. Out of the corner of his eye, he noted that the girl was crouched into a tight ball.

Colonel Windburn drummed his fingers on his desk; he was deep in thought. The mission had begun, but things had gone seriously wrong. There had been no word from the two SAS squadrons, and now the Air Mountains were alive with volcanic activity. This had been the only contingency left open to him; also it was his greatest fear. The office door opened; he looked up as a handwritten communiqué was placed on his desk. Scanning the report, it seemed that the mission had been a success, but at what cost, the Colonel wondered.

There were no survivors. The eruption of the mountain had swept everything away. Two squadrons, sixty-four men, now dead, the Colonel thought.

The human instigation of awakening Mother Nature would have its own ramifications for years to come, but these acts outweighed the potential of a developing country claiming nuclear weapons. All they could do now was offer aid.

Chapter 22

The helicopter headed in an easterly direction, leaving the devastation of the Air Mountains behind them. Graham Harrington was in an inexplicable frame of mind; the dead thing had removed the muzzle of the weapon from his head, but still maintained its possession.

Ahead of them lay the great expanse of the Tenere Desert. In the distance, a mere smear across the horizon, was the Djado Plateau with its ravaged villages. As they traversed the barren terrain, the helicopter maintained a low altitude mere feet from the ground. Kerry peered at the corpse; her silence indicated that she had gone into some kind of shock. Her eyes wide open, staring, she looked to be removed from everything except the corpse.

'Jack!' she said, with a monotone dullness to her voice. The zombie maintained indifference.

The helicopter seemed void and airless, Graham listening intently. Kerry's eyes became circumspect and comprehending.

'You want revenge on me?'

There was a sudden buffeting of the craft, and it veered skyward at an increasing speed. Leaving behind a trail of oily, black smoke, the craft began to cough and stutter. The helicopter peaked and came to a virtual standstill in the air before plummeting back towards the ground. Graham frantically fought the controls, lights blinking before his eyes as a warning siren sounded. His face was bathed in sweat, and he viewed a daunting scene before him.

He felt something crash into the back of his seat, but gave it little thought, his concentration devoted to restarting the engine. The engine stuttered into life, and the rotors began to whirl, gathering speed. Straining with all his muscles, Graham pulled back the control stick, feeling a slight give in their descent, allowing him to coax the helicopter back into a standard flying position.

The ground below was hard-baked and encrusted with jagged rocks; running between these rocks were ragged, intertwining fissures that expanded into gaping breaches and disjunctions. It was a desolate landscape that appeared as unforgiving as it was alien.

A rending and twisting sound resounded from the rear, and the helicopter tilted forward onto its nose, coming into direct contact with the surface. The rotor blades cut into the ground, churning up the surface before it. The helicopter flipped onto its roof as the rotor blades were torn from the craft. The surviving cockpit became a rotating roller coaster.

The wreck of the helicopter finally came to a standstill. Graham felt something snap and twist in his chest. The pain was unbearable, threatening to drag him into unconsciousness. His eyes flickered open onto a world that had a dusty, blanched appearance. Rays of sunlight filtered through a torn and ravaged fuselage, and, looking down, Graham saw a pair of soiled feet. He called out for help, but the noise that he made was a rasp that culminated in death.

Kerry opened her eyes. She felt a pounding in her temple and she was dazed and confused as she surveyed her surroundings. Moving caused pain throughout her body, and a thread of blood crept down her cheek from her temple. She smelt fuel.

Climbing to her feet, she frantically sought an exit, her fear mounting to a crescendo of hysteria as she saw the dangling figure of the pilot. From what she could see, he was dead. Then she recollected Jack, or rather the abomination that Jack had become.

Steadily the cockpit began to fill with smoke, and Kerry saw a rent, the gap just wide enough for her to climb through. She leapt for the opening, her arm catching on something jagged. Feeling her skin tear, she landed heavily on the hard-baked desert floor, breathing in the hot air. Coughing, she gasped for breath. When the seizure passed, she gazed out upon an arid and unforgiving scene. There was desert sand everywhere, as far as the eye could see. The sandbanks formed gigantic dunes that reached to the sky.

She was lost and alone; then, from the corner of her eye, she spotted a small boy wearing nothing more than a loincloth. He stood regarding her, grinning; there was something bright about his smile. She watched him walk towards the ravaged remains of Jack. The boy displayed no fear as he approached the zombie.

He turned, waving at her, and she watched him take hold of the dead thing's hand. She felt pain in her right arm, and on further investigation discovered there was a nasty gash in her forearm. Tearing a piece of material from her blouse, she secured a binding, stemming the flow of blood, her attention returning to the boy.

Watching them, Kerry realised she was alone, with no one to help her. Her only salvation lay in following the boy and the corpse. She displayed caution, following at a safe distance behind, when a sudden whoosh reverberated into the stillness behind her. Looking back, she saw the burning wreckage of the helicopter. The flames licked at the fuselage with a greedy and insatiable appetite. There was a sudden rush of air and an ear-shattering explosion. Kerry was pitched backward, the heat of the flames scorching her face.

The sun beat down with ferocity. Kerry lay motionless on the sand, her limbs aching, her mind numb. Vaguely, she remembered some sort of crash: who or what it involved she had no recollection of. In the distance, she saw movement, two figures trekking across the desert; other survivors, her desperate mind told her. She felt saved. Calling out, she broke into a run.

It was not long before she realised her folly. Her arm was bleeding again, her legs felt like leaden weights and she collapsed to her knees, seeing in front of her a conical hill that wavered in the heat. Buildings surrounded the mound. The ancient and ramshackle dwellings looked to be deserted, but the scene renewed hope in her heart. Climbing shakily to her feet, Kerry found a new resolve and she headed towards her shimmering salvation.

Chapter 23

Kerry faltered across the desert waste. The naked land was still, without a gasp of air to be felt. The ground was parched, and Kerry viewed the hill loom nearer with every step. She imagined a draught of cool air was blowing across a sandy beach. A haze impinged her vision, a silvery shimmer of heat she imagined to be the waves of the sea. She yearned for the caress of water lapping at her feet, but, as she staggered nearer, desiring to soothe her scorched limbs, the mirage dissolved before her eyes as if it had never been. It was replaced with a festering dryness that gathered tightly around her.

As she staggered towards the mound, the hill had been in plain view, but in her hallucinatory state she must have wandered off course, because now, poised before her, were dunes and drifts of sand of immense proportion. These gigantic sand walls stood some hundred feet above her head. Her mind reeled in abandonment. Death would now be the easy way out, and for Kerry O'Moore the easy way out had never been an option.

Turning in panic, she spied the hill climbing out of the sands. It appeared to be a primitive city that was now a mere vestige of its former glory. Two silhouettes stood motionless in the distance.

The ruins of this once majestic city were a place well suited to what the rotting remains of Jack Hornsby had come to personify. The city represented death in its decayed and destitute state. Kerry watched the silhouettes move into the base of the ruined city. Willing herself forward, a dry rasp dogged her throat. The ruins had become her last monument of hope.

Her desire to survive became a steel-edged sword. Every feeble step was a step closer, her thirst pushing her to resist the enshrouding bleakness of doom hovering above.

They entered the city, a city constructed of hardened mud, blanched white from the incessant glare of an unrelenting sun. Passageways formed a labyrinth, connecting the layered rooms that had been constructed around the hill.

Both boy and corpse wound their way into the dead city, following these narrow passageways and intertwining paths, coming to a standstill before an empty room.

As if he had been formed of the very darkness itself, Samdi appeared before them.

'I knew you would come!' the Bokor declared, in a grave and suspicious voice. 'It was only a matter of time!' His eyes were illuminated with a hidden knowledge that transcended the ages. He regarded the zombie. 'And you brought my tool.'

The boy regarded him. 'Someone had to stop you, Father!'

'You always were strong and the *Loa* remain strong in you. The *Orisha* stand in judgement of me, but they are also afraid: afraid of what I will become, afraid of what I have attained!'

The boy was unmoved. Tilting his head to one side, he studied his father. 'You must realise that the *Orisha* will not allow this to happen. The balance between good and evil must remain! No mortal can aspire to be a god. The forces of good and evil will not allow this. I plead with you to change your course, for this will only lead to folly! Father, you know what must be done. The great spirits that watch over all of creation are allowing you this last chance at redemption. If you wish to honour yourself and me, then you must perform the ritual of spiritual release before it is too late!'

Samdi stood in reflection for a time, before saying, 'Yes, you are right!' He bowed his head, speaking carefully with an even and subdued tone. 'You will follow me!'

He led them further into the abandoned city. The boy and the zombie trailed behind. The boy could not see the Bokor's face. Samdi wore a smile that told of his vicious intent.

Kerry floundered into the primordial city. It was only a few hundred years ago that this primitive metropolis had been vibrant with life. It had been abandoned due to hordes of raiding Touaregs and western slave hunters that raped the once proud city.

Djado was now a crumbling conurbation of phantoms. Venturing into the labyrinth of passageways, she was drawn by her rasping thirst. Falling, she had little strength to go any further. Then she saw a hole in the ground, nothing more than a primitive well, but it was enough to raise hope. Sliding forward on her belly, she tried to moisten her dried and cracked lips with her tongue.

Peering into the hole, below was a black void of uncertain dimensions. The well could have dried up years before, becoming nothing more than a hiding place for vipers and scorpions, but her nagging thirst urged her on. Kerry reached down, her mind shielded against the inevitable strike of a snake or insect. She had stretched her arm in as far as her shoulder when her hand hit the water. The contrast was stark, almost painful. Trying to scoop it in the cup of her hand, most of the water filtered away through her fingers. She lapped eagerly at her moistened palm. The water tasted strange.

Kerry heard a pounding, a rhythmic beat that nagged at her. She realised that the pounding was coming from beneath her! The ground was alive with a steady beat. Fear gripped her, and she shuddered, remembering the Air Mountains. Climbing to her feet, she was aware that the pounding vibrated through the very air itself.

The ancient city was deserted, but Kerry felt that she was not alone. There were openings leading off from the corridors. The darkness contained within was blacker than pitch, tangible where the bleakness held form. Talking to herself, she tried to muster courage.

Something was lying on the ground, and she saw it was a crude doll. Not knowing why, she stooped down, examining it. It was an effigy wrapped in a snake skin, and Kerry recognised it as that of Phillip Égalité, complete with white fedora.

Chapter 24

Samdi led the way, their progress accompanied by the sound of drums. The Bokor was smiling as thoughts of his ascension ran through his mind.

'Fools! Do they believe that I will forsake my standing, now that I have almost completed my aim? I am a god! I possess the power of the immortals! And I will not be denied my rightful destiny, even by my own blood!'

They continued to ascend the hill, an oppressive atmosphere surrounding them; it pressed down, almost hemming them in. The sound of drums grew louder, pulsating with an increased tempo. They exited the city, fast approaching the summit of the hill.

Standing before a huge, unlit fire, the Bokor came to a standstill at its base. Producing a rolled parchment from a knapsack, he turned to face the zombie and the boy, his face full of sorrow.

'And so it has come to this!' he said. His expression rapidly evaporated to be replaced by a face of purest evil. 'On this parchment lie the answers to questions man has asked since time immemorial. A cure for death! It has taken me all my life to discover the secrets of life and death. I have searched in lands far and wide, discovered cultures that you believe are merely myth. I have dedicated my life to this, and you expect me to throw it all away?' He issued a cruel and callous laugh that boomed into the surrounding air.

The figure of a man in a white suit walked from the back of the unlit pyre. His suit was soiled. 'This is the man who tried to enslave me. Égalité discovered, much to his discomfort, that I in return enslaved him. A malign spirit now inhabits his body. A *Baka*! A demon summoned from the underworld to take possession of a host. The *Baka* is an eater of human flesh. It is now devouring Mr Égalité from the inside. Make no mistake, this demon possesses great power. A power which I now control!'

Égalité stood motionless before them, his eyes a vivid yellow. Rifts emerged, transposing his pupils, exhuming a sense of endless evil.

'You must stop this!'

Samdi regarded the boy's outcry with contempt, his mind set upon one thing: power. Samdi turned his attention to the zombie.

'It is I that now controls the corpse!' he said.

'The *Orisha* control it,' the boy corrected.

The zombie took a step forward as the attention of Égalité fell upon it.

Samdi tried to exert his force of will over the animated corpse, his intrusion being thrust back. The corpse began to glow, filled with a blinding light that banished the darkness within. It was imbued with the power of the *Orisha*. Sensing the power that had taken control of Jack, Samdi cringed away.

Kerry stumbled through the city. She held the voodoo doll wrapped in the snake skin in her hand. She was creating illusions in her own mind. One fantasy scenario led to another, until Kerry was finding a strange solace in the creations of her own imagination.

She halted abruptly, tentatively looking around her. Seeing movement up ahead, there was a sudden change in atmosphere; it became subdued and weighted. Her hand felt warm, and she looked down at the doll she carried in her hand. The image was horrific to look upon, and Kerry didn't know why she had kept hold of it; she felt loath to discard it. It was as though the graven image had become moulded to her hand.

Moving onward, Kerry continued to wind her way up the hill. She was following the sounds of drums, the beat her guide. Kerry felt movement in her hand, it was fluid and alive. Her mind told her not to look, but her curiosity got the better of her. To her horror, she discovered the wooden doll had transformed into a live, writhing snake. The serpent coiled its way around her arm. Repulsed, she threw the serpent aside, relieving the mounting terror that swelled inside her. But the combination of fatigue and shock hindered her escape. When Kerry came to a standstill, she discovered to her relief that she had broken free of the dismal corridors, and had come to the summit of the hill. A little way ahead, Kerry saw the boy standing just in front of Jack's zombie.

Two other people were with them; the first was Samdi, wearing tribal clothing of an eccentric design. The second person was Égalité. Kerry stopped.

The zombie took a step forward to find its path blocked by Égalité. Already a transformation was beginning to occur; his skin, virtually transparent, was beginning to shed. Beneath the paper-thin visage, a form could be seen. The entity resembled a serpent, and, as the skin began to tear, the hideous form emerged from its human pupa. The creature had the flat head of a cobra and bat-like wings sprouted from its back. Its arms ended in deadly talons, and a tail extended from the back, adding stability to this terrible lizard. It hissed, bringing forward the cowl on its head, dripping a poisonous substance from curved and wicked teeth. The creature was a demon of nightmares. Moving forward to meet its challenge, the Baka spat its venom, the fluid eating away the rotting tissue of the zombie's face. The zombie grasped the creature, a white light leaving its hand. The light quickly encompassed the demon, turning it to dust.

The Jack-thing turned its attention to Samdi, moving towards him. It was brought to a sudden halt.

'Not even the might of the *Orisha* have the power to stop me!' The cadaver of Jack was flung backwards.

'I warned you, Father!' the boy shouted.

From the ground, dark shadows emerged, twisting and writhing, their visages gaping into demonic maws that screamed with vengeful intent. The shadows encircled Samdi, engulfing him, before rushing toward the zombie, disappearing into its form.

The zombie sat up, the Bokor staring at it, when the boy said, 'Face your accuser, Father!'

Samdi looked upon the face of *Oludumare*, the chief god of the Yoruba people. Faltering, he almost fell upon his knees. The corpse blazed with a blinding brilliance. The light diminished, as the corpse of Jack Hornsby became imbued by the spirits of the *Orisha*. The unlit pyre exploded, green flames devouring the dry wood. The zombie advanced towards him.

Samdi looked into the face of death as the corpse grasped him, lifting him high above its head. Lifeless fingers caressed his temple; eyes, frozen and unseeing, regarded him.

The dark shades congregated around the boy, vanishing as though they had never been. The zombie turned as the flames from the fire reached out to it…

Jack perceived the phantoms of life. The light was distant, but getting closer, pushing back the darkness and dissolving it. Before him stood the *Orishas*, the *Zanj* of heaven and sky. Their number was indefinite, far too many for Jack's psyche to fully comprehend, but he perceived that they were all part of the same whole.

He saw Lisa standing there waiting for him… Then the light took him and he felt at peace.

Running, Kerry fled through the earthen city; the narrow passageways pressed in on her. She saw more of them: the dead, standing motionless, waiting. Stumbling, she fell forward, her head hitting the ground hard. Dazed, she forced herself up, glancing behind where an unholy horde had gathered, their unfeeling hands reaching out towards her. She ran, racing beyond the boundaries of the city, out into the darkening desert. The night was cruel and relentless in its arrival. She didn't know how far she had travelled; she was hungry and thirsty. With nothing but a cold moon to keep her company, she collapsed on the ground, waiting for death to take her.

Waking, she saw a relentless sun high in the sky. Climbing to her feet, she spotted the earthen city not more than a mile away. Weary and tired, she ran a dry tongue across parched lips. Had she imagined the whole thing? She could see the wreckage of the helicopter lying in the distance. Had she crawled from the wreckage shocked and been wandering around aimlessly for days? Peering into the heat-hazed desert, she saw someone moving.

Elation rose in her heart and she headed out to meet them. It must be the pilot, she thought. The figure loitered, seemingly lost, then bent down. As Kerry neared, she saw it was a man, wearing tattered trousers and combat top.

'Hey, Graham! I'm so glad to see you!' Kerry cried, as the man stopped what he was doing, deliberately turning round. Kerry gasped in horror, backing away. The zombie's face was seared to the bone. The undead creature opened its mouth in a rictus of a smile. Kerry began to scream, only to be confronted by an archaic city of the damned.

The zombies surrounded her, and Kerry had no means of escape. A coarse, guttural laugh rose on the tide of the wind, and Samdi separated himself from the masses. She could see a twisted and self-satisfied smile on his face.

'We all have to pay the reaper sometime!' he said.

Kerry began to scream uncontrollably as the living dead moved in for the kill…

Printed in the United Kingdom
by Lightning Source UK Ltd.
132715UK00001B/30/A